BM

A MAN NAMED DUNDEE

A MAN NAMED DUNDEE

LEO P. KELLEY

Doubleday
NEW YORK
1988

All of the characters in this book
are fictitious, and any resemblance
to actual persons, living or dead,
is purely coincidental.

Library of Congress Cataloging-in-Publication Data

Kelley, Leo P.
A man named Dundee.

I. Title.
PS3561.E388M36   1988   813'.54   87-27181

JUBAL BONNER'S MEMOIRS: AN INTRODUCTION

Jubal Bonner's memoirs, published here for the first time, were written in 1865. They might never have appeared in print had it not been for the recent publication of another book: *Major James Parkinson, A Life* by Robert Baskin.

The Bonner memoirs were submitted to the publisher by Lawrence Dundee, the great-grandson of the man who was known to Jubal Bonner only as Dundee and who figures prominently in the memoirs. Lawrence Dundee, in his letter to us which accompanied the memoirs, wrote in part:

The Bonner memoirs have been treasured by the Dundee family ever since they first came into my great-grandfather's possession. No one in the family, to the best of my knowledge, has ever considered offering them for publication before.

However, the appearance of Mr. Robert Baskin's laudatory but, unfortunately, grossly inaccurate account of certain events which occurred late in the life of Major Parkinson and the false accusations against Jubal Bonner which his book contains now prompts me to place the memoirs in your hands in the hope that you will want to publish them.

Should you decide to do so, you will have helped to set the historical record straight, something Mr. Baskin has not done primarily because he has relied on inaccurate sources for information such as the newspaper, The Advocate, *which he cites repeatedly. I know my great-grandfather, were he alive today, would very much want to see that historical record corrected so that readers might learn the truth about certain events which took place during the bloody border wars of 1865.*

The memoirs have not been altered, except to divide them into paragraphs and chapters for the convenience of the modern reader. Otherwise, they are presented here exactly as they were written by Jubal Bonner.

A MAN NAMED DUNDEE

CHAPTER 1

A man named Dundee is who I am going to write about.

Dundee was the only name I ever knew him by. That was what folk all called him. Just Dundee.

Ever sinse I have been in this cell and even during my Tryal I have thought a whole lot about him. Somewheres along the way I taken the notion to write down what I know about him. It helps to pass the time. It also helps me to keep my mind off how Hell bent they are on hanging me ever sinse the Judge and Jury called me guilty.

I remember the day I met Dundee for the first time like it was Yesterday. He was sitting on the ground next his fire and looking at nothing but not missing nothing neither I could tell when I rode up and seen the beans he had boiling and the Coffee pot steeming in his fire.

He didnt look up at me and he didnt say a thing. He just sit there and I recollect how he looked to me like a Cougar getting set to spring. He sit there easy enough but you could tell he was reddy and able to make his move if you went and rubbed him the wrong way. I didnt want to do that so I said howdy just as frendly as ever I knew how to.

He looked straight up at me and all of a sudden I could see what he was seeing like it was all reflekted there in those crowblack eyes of his which was taking me in and somehow keeping me from moving so much as a mussle. What he seen was a youngun who was stretching out of his clothes but one that had not yet got his full growth. A youngun that was all Bones with not much meat on them underneeth clothes that had sure seen better days. I could feel myself getting skittish with the way he was studying me and him all the time staying as silent as a Stone. You couldnt tell what was on his mind and maybe I got to thinking that was all to the good.

Then he looked away from me and I felt like he had just turned me loose. I reckoned I wasnt wanted or welcome so I turned my horse and started to move on down the vallee when he said all of a sudden the Coffee is strong and the beans is hot and your welcome to a share.

By that time I wasnt so sure I wanted any part of him. I had seen the sidearm he had in a holster hung on a belt strapped around his Waist. I had also seen the double bareled breech loading brush gun he had in the Saddle Boot on his black gelding. Then there was those eyes of his like I said before. They peerced you like knifes. His strong and rough edged voice had a way of sometimes sending shivers up and down your Spine. He was dark complekted and his hair was straight and black. It was almost as long as an Indians. His lips was thin and I remember thinking they looked like they had forgot how to smile a long time ago. You could tell he was tall even though he was sitting crosslegged on the ground in front of his fire. He looked to me Dundee did like he could eat nails for brekfast and have himself a second helping.

He didn't say nothing else so I reckoned the next

move was up to me. I got off my horse and went over
to his fire. I hunkered down more than a spitting
distance away from him and said I am much obliged
for the invite. He didnt say a thing. So I said my name
is Jubal Bonner who might you be.

My name is Dundee he said and proseeded to spoon
some beans onto a tin Plate which he handed to me.

I come from Kentucky I told him and I am heading
west.

Why he asked me and then he poured me a cup of
Coffee.

I just plain didnt have any idea about how to anser
his Question though I did give it some real hard
thought. I thought about Mr. Murkin. I thought about
what might be waiting on me out west and how I was
chomping at the bit to get to where whatever it was
was at.

Dundee give me a straight on look and said man or
boy a Fellow ought to know why he does what he does.

I stuffed some beans into my mouth and washed
them down with some Coffee. I desided to turn the
tables on him. Where are you headed is what I asked
him then.

Have you run off from home he asked me without
never once ansering my Question.

I shook my head and he give me another one of those
straight on looks of his and I knew for sure and right
away that he knew I was lieing. Which was true I was.
I had run off from the homeplace. I had put up with
things about as long as I could. About a year after Pa
dyed Ma went and married Mr. Murkin. Things
wasnt ever the same again after that. Not for her and
not for me. Mr. Murkin was a drinking man. Not
steady but he went at the Corn at leest once a Week.

When he taken to drinking he also taken to fighting with anybody what come close to him which most of the time ment Ma or me or like as not both of us at the selfsame time. Ma put up with it as best she could. He is really not a meen man at Heart she would tell me from time to time when she saw I was down in the dumps. Its the drink. It does bad things to some men. It makes them hateful. He is One of them it harms.

I tryed my best to stop Mr. Murkin from hitting Ma but all I got for my trouble was a split lip once and black eyes more times than I could count on the fingers of both hands.

It was Mr. Murkin who put Ma in an early Grave. The granny woman who tended her there at the end said it was Pleurisy killed her. I say it was Mr. Murkin. The day Ma died it was me buried her. Mr. Murkin taken off for the hills long before she give out with her last gasp. When he come on back down out of the high country Three days later I knew right off he had been to the still the Krendells run east of Compton crick on account of how he was riproaring drunk and looking for to fight. When he went for me I was reddy for him. I hit him hard as I could. He let out a bellow like a Bull that has been kept from the Cows and come at me again. I stood my ground and hit him again. This time I put him down on the ground. I didnt say nothing to him. I just stood there. He got up and said well at leest somebody in the family has got guts. That made me wild. I went for him and drunk as he was he never stood a chanse against the way my Blood was boiling like fire in my veins and my Fists was smashing and smashing into him one right after the other like they never would stop till the Last Trump.

But they did stop. It seemed to me like I had been

beating on Mr. Murkin for an Hour but it was more
than likely only Five minnits maybe Six. I left him
lieing on the ground and walked off knowing I would
never have to set eyes on him ever again. I kept on
walking and pretty soon it got dark. I slept that first
night in a barn I come across. Next day was more of
the same. Walking with the sun at my back to start
with but up in front of me as the day wore on so I
could follow it to wherever it was I was going.

I worked here and there. I helped a blacksmith for a
spell in one town. I hayed for a farmer. Along the way
I got myself the buckskin I was riding when I come
upon Dundee.

He didnt say any more about me running off from
the homeplace. I said it sure is a nice day the sun is as
hot as a full fired oven. He said rain is on the way. I
looked up at the sky that had not a cloud in it and then
sidelong at him and he said the chickweeds closed its
leaves.

I can see that I said as I looked at the chickweed he
had pointed to. Does that meen rain I asked him. He
nodded and pointed to the tails of our horses. There
tails look as big as bushes he said. That is on account of
the hairs in there tails are all standing up. That there is
another sign that meens rain is on the way.

Now I never knew that before. I mean about how
chickweed and horses tails do before it starts in to rain.
To tell the truth I found it hard to believe in at the
time on account of how the sun was shining and there
was not a cloud to be seen in the sky.

An Hour later it started in to rain. Five minutes
after it did it was pouring buckets and I was drenshed
to the Skin. But Dundee was as dry as an old Bone. He
had put on a long yellow slicker before the rain

started. I helped him pack up. There was no need to put out the cook fire. The rain did that.

I am heading due west Dundee told me. I am to I said as he swung into his Saddle. I did the same and when he moved out so did I. I kept a little bit behind him on account of I wasnt exactly sure if he minded me tagging along with him or not. We rode through the rain with neither one of us talking. The rain poured off the brim of his hat but all it did was soak into mine till the felt was all soggy and hanging down around my ears. It kept on like that for a good two hours. Then it slowed down some and then it stopped. Water dripped down from the trees and the ground was bogged up pretty bad. Every time my buckskin lifted up a hoof it made a kind of sucking sound on account of the way the mud was everywhere.

Dundee never once looked back over his shoulder to see was I still there behind him or not. Could be he didnt know I was tagging along behind him.

I was a far peese from dry by the time he stopped. He got off his horse and took off his slicker and set to making camp for the night. He didnt ask me to help him but I did. I went hunting wood and what I found I brought back to start a fire with.

That wood is no good he told me. Its been laying on the ground and it has soaked up too much water. Even in dry wether wood you get off the ground wont make a good fire. Its too smoky and slow burning.

I said all the wood around here is wet. What is wrong with a smoky fire. We can sit on the side of it the wind is blowing from.

He paid me no mind. He went into the woods and started hacking off some tree branches with a big knife he had. He brought them back and split some of them into sticks no more than an inch thick. He made a little teepee out of them and then he took a wooden Match from a tin can he carryed and lit it. In no time he had a hot cook fire going.

Smoke from a fire tells folk where you are he said only it seemed like he was talking to himself. You might as well send out invitations as start a smoky fire. Unless you happen to like company. The trouble with company though is you never know who you might get.

I put Coffee in the pot and filled it at a crick that wasnt far off and put the pot on the fire. Dundee took it off. What did I do wrong I asked him.

Nothing he said. I got to go get us some supper. Game holes up when it rains. But critters will be coming out to forage now before it gets to dark for them. He took his brush gun out his Saddle Boot and off he went into the woods.

I went after him. He didnt say go back when he seen me so I stuck right with him. We walked for a spell but didnt see or hear anything. Then Dundee said listen. I listened. He said over there. I looked over to where he was looking but I didnt see anything. The sound of his shot made my ears ring.

He went and got the jack I had never even seen but he had shot and then we started back to camp. Along the way I spotted a squirrel. I eyed it and it eyed me. Then I looked up at Dundee and saw how he was watching me.

You want to try to take that critter he asked me. I told him I didnt have no gun. He loaded and handed over his. I tryed holding it real steddy in both hands but still I missed that squirrel when I pulled the trigger and it sitting there without making a move. I handed his gun back to Dundee. He didnt say a word. I wouldnt let myself dwell on what he might be thinking.

That night we had roasted rabbit for supper. All the while I was eating it I kept thinking about how my Pa had dyed when I was but a tad so he never had a chanse to teech me how to shoot. He was a crakerjack shot my Pa was. If he had shot at that squirrel I seen he wouldnt have missed it the way I did. That poor critter never would have known what hit him. Same as the jack Dundee shot didnt.

Next day when I woken Dundee was nowhere in sight. I sit up quick and looked all around for him. When I seen his horse was still tyed next to mine I breathed a little bit easier. I had pulled on my Boots and was clapping my hat on my head when he came moseying out of the woods buttoning up his pants.

He told me to build a fire. I borroed his knife and cut some branches from some trees to start it with. We ate what was left of the jack and drunk Coffee. Then Dundee started getting his horse reddy to ride. After I cleaned up and kicked out the fire I did the same.

We rode out with me thinking how we had never even said so much as good day to each other. Build a fire Dundee had said to me is all. Like he didnt have time or any use for frendly talk. He sure was a sollem sort of man. Ever sinse I run into him I had not once seen a smile on his face. He put me in mind of a man who has hurtful things on his mind and wont open his mouth any more than he has to for fear he might give in and start talking to somebody about them. I know that was the way I was when Pa dyed. And even more so after Ma went and married Mr. Murkin. I just didnt say one more word than I had to to nobody.

We rode west through Missouri. Dundee had a way of sitting nice and easy in the Saddle which I tryed to imitate only every time I did I near to fell off my horse. I still dont know how he did it.

We was crossing a plain with mountains running from east to west off on our right when Dundee drew rein.

I allmost asked him what for was we stopping. But I didnt. I knew him good enough by now to know he would tell me if he thought I ought to know. If he didnt he just wouldnt say nothing leaving me to try to figure him out which was no easy thing to do.

Covered Wagon coming I told him when I spotted it up ahead of us. Then I felt like a fool for saying that on account of I reckon he seen the Wagon before I did and that was why he had reined in his horse. We sat our Saddles watching the Wagon come closer and closer. I give Dundee a sidelong look and seen how hard he was squinting at it. A man was driving it. When he drove up alongside us he said whoa to his team and threw on the brake. Good morning he said looking down at Dundee but not smiling.

Good day to you Dundee said back.

I seen the way the two of them was sizing each other up. The Wagon driver said he was heading east which was plain enough for anybody to see. He said he couldnt get to where he was going fast enough to suit him.

That so Dundee said.

We are going to Tennessee the Wagon driver said. My wife has her a sister there.

Your wife is anxious to see her sister is she Dundee said.

Yes and no the Wagon driver said.

Dundee waited for him to say some more.

Back there where we just come from is pure Hell with the lid off the Wagon driver said.

Back where I wondered.

I heard there was trouble brewing on the border Dundee said.

Its done been brewed the Wagon driver said. Trouble he said is to mild a word for it.

Just then a woman stuck her head out the Wagon and give first Dundee and then me big smiles. She said good morning to us and then she told the Wagon driver the children were hungry and could they stop here for brekfast. He said sure they could. Then he invited Dundee and me to have brekfast with them.

That is kindly of you Dundee said. We will.

Which surprised me on account of how we had allreddy had brekfast and I for one had no room for any more.

The woman climbed down out the Wagon with a boy about Six and a girl about Eight in tow. I am Missus Soames she said and these are my children Amy and Edward. You have allreddy met my husband. She said his name is Will.

My name is Dundee maam Dundee said. He touched the brim of his hat to her nice and polite. The boy there his name is Jubal Bonner.

Pleased to meet you both I told the Soameses and then they all got busy making a cook fire and getting brekfast with Dundee and me helping however we could. I told them not to use wood from the ground or they would get more smoke than flame from there fire and so Mister Soames broke a branch from a tree with a ax he had and we used that.

Pretty soon Missus Soames passed out china plates

to us. Each one was heeped high with salt pork Rice turnips and dumplings with peeses of dryed apple in them.

I looked at Dundee and he was forking food into his mouth like a starving man. In between bites he told Missus Soames that she sure did know how to cook good eats. She said thank you sir its nice of you to say so. I try my best.

Before I knew it I was staring down at my empty plate which proved the truth of what Dundee had just said about Missus Soameses cooking.

You look like your near to your time Dundee told her.

I could feel my face going red. But Dundee never turned a hair though Missus Soames put her eyes down and folded her hands over her swollen belly. If its a girl we are going to name her Ida she said real shy and if its a boy Bill.

Back there in Clay county these days is no place to try to raise a family Mister Soames said. So we pulled up stakes. We plan to settle some place else that is peesefull.

A man has to look after his family to see that they stay safe Dundee said as he taken the china cup full of Coffee Missus Soames handed him.

That is the gospel Truth Mister Soames said. Back in Clay county a Persons life aint worth a plugged nickel with all those Kansas Jayhawkers scouring the country worse than Ten Plegs of Locusts. Those old boys maim and kill and pillage and burn like they was Satans own avengers. And the Southern Sympathizers in Missouri is as bad.

Missus Soames heeved a sigh and said none of them

can be said to lead Christian lives. They do not turn the other cheek nor do they follow the Golden Rool.

Mister Soames said what happens is a bunch of bad Missouri boys rides over the border into Kansas and raises Cane there and then they skedaddle back to Missouri. Next thing you know you have got Jayhawkers coming out of Kansas and crossing over the border and raising Cane in Missouri. The first bunch claims to be fighting for the Confederacy and the second bunch for the Union.

The War is over Dundee said.

Not for those Fellows its not Mister Soames said. They are still fighting it tooth and nail.

I dont think it is a matter of the South versus the North Missus Soames said. That is just an ekscuse which allows renegades on both sides of the issue to cloak themselves in Patriotism. But there real aim and only goal is plunder. And wurse. She blushed when she said that last part.

The three of them went right on talking and I just sit there and listened. Mister Soames said things was bad on the border and getting wurse. Missus Soames said how she had hated to leave her homeplace on account of how it was where Mister Soames taken her on the day they was marryed. He built the homested with his own two hands she said and I seen the pride in her face when she said it.

Edward and Amy kept as quiet as me. They kept looking at Dundee and then at me and then back at him again as if the two of us was about to pownse on them.

Dundee did a lot of listening and not much talking. I notised how he didnt ask any Questions. But the things he said or maybe it was the way he said them

got Mister Soames and his Missus to open up till the
two of them was chattering away like Magpies. I could
see how he managed to learn all there was to know
without seeming to pry into the Soameses personal
lives. They seemed to like to tell him things. I reckon
it was on account of the way he showed an interest in
each One of them. Like when he told Missus Soames
he had never seen such handsom children when to tell
you the Truth Edward looked to me a little like a Wulf
and Amy well the kindest thing you could say about
her was she was plain.

Before long though the Soameses started asking
Dundee Questions. When he started ansering them I
perked up my ears.

Missus Soames started off by asking him where he
was traveling to.

I am heading home he told her.

She asked him where his home was at.

He said Jackson county Missouri.

Mister Soames got a dark look on his face then. He
said Union Sympathizers are raiding all over Jackson
county. Same as up where we come from in Clay
county he said. Even on down into Cass and Bates
countys to he said.

Have you been away from home very long Missus
Soames asked Dundee.

His voice was low when he told her allmost Four
years.

She looked at her husband. He looked at Dundee
and said I guess maybe you was in the War.

I was Dundee said.

I am so glad its over Missus Soames said. I cant abide
killing. In that awful War it was brothers hand raised
against brother.

Looks like you come through it in one peese Mister Soames said.

Dundee didnt say a word.

Mister Soames asked Dundee which side he fought on. I thought at first Dundee wasnt going to anser him but finally he did. He looked off into the distance for a minnit and then he said the South.

Along about that time Mister Soames looked around and then he told Edward and Amy to start cleaning up they had a long way yet to go and the day was getting older by the minnit.

They did as they was bid and Missus Soames fussed some with her dress and then she asked Dundee did he want some more Coffee. He said no thank you maam. She said she was sure glad the War was all over and the killing at an end.

Only it aint her husband said. Which is why we packed up and left Clay county like I said before. Those Fellows back there on both sides are still using the war to fatten there own purses with plunder.

And to satisfy there sinful appetites his Missus said in a kind of whisper.

Dundee walked away like he wanted to be by himself for a spell. When he was gone Missus Soames said to me he is not a very talkative man is he. I said no maam he sure enough isnt.

He is a hard man isnt he she asked me.

He does seem so I said.

Are you going with him to his homeplace she asked me.

I shook my head.

Oh she said. I thought the two of you were heading for the same destination.

I am on my way out west I told her.

She looked over at her Son and I seen the sad look
on her face. I suppose all boys of a certain age have a
hankering to see the world she said.

I for one do I allowed.

Didnt your folk mind when you left them she asked
me.

There dead I told her.

She put out a hand and touched my cheek. So young
she said. So young to be all alone and on your own in
this wicked world.

I am not alone I told her. I am with Dundee.

But after the Soameses had gone and Dundee and
me were riding on I got to thinking about what I had
said to Missus Soames about me being with Dundee. I
wasnt all that sure when I turned it over in my mind if
that was the Truth or not. I meen I was with him
allright but I didnt have a feeling that I really was
most of the time. I had the feeling that he was all alone
and never mind about me riding there right alongside
of him.

He was that kind of man. He didnt seem to need
nobody. Or want nobody neither. It showed in the
way he didnt talk much. He was a man kept his own
council. I wished more than once though that he
would open up and talk about the wether or
something. Or the War he was in and what he did in it.
But no. Not Dundee. He just rode along with his
hands folded around his Saddle Horn and his Boots
planted in his stirrups and his eyes roving all over.

We had gone a few miles through woods that was
chock full of brambles before I said to him you took
me by surprise back there saying you would take
brekfast with the Soameses when you had allreddy had
brekfast. I guess you was still hungry.

I wasnt he said.

Which surprised me all over again. Then what for did you say you would stay and take brekfast I asked him.

He said when I heard Soames say he was from the Missouri border I thought I ought to hear what he might have to say about what was going on back there where I come from. I reckoned I might profit from hearing the man out.

After a while I said I guess your glad the War is over. He didnt say nothing to that so I said I had a powerful hankering to go join the army but I was way to young. They would have sent me packing after telling me I could come on back once I had growed up into a man. I laughed but Dundee didnt.

He said some Fellows dont know when there well off.

I said do you meen to say that I was well off not joining the army and helping to fight the War.

War is not all fansee Uniforms and bugle calls and Banners flying he said.

I was still wondering what he ment by that when he said War is no Sunday School picnic.

I said I reckon its not.

He gave me a black look and said old men deside there going to have themselves a War but its the young men who have to die in it. When its over not a whole lot has changed. One side wins and one side loses is all. Time moves on. Folk start in to forgetting about what started the whole thing in the first place. A man that was your Enemy yesterday turns out to be your friend tomorrow. But that dont bring back the dead.

From what the Soamses had to say I said it sounds like the War is still going on back where you come

from. Do you reckon will those Jayhawkers cause you
any trouble when you get there I asked him.

My fighting days are done he said. I have no quarrel
with the men who are raising Hell on the border.
They can tend to there business and I will tend to
mine. That way we wont get in each others hair.

I asked him was his homeplace a nice one. I
reckoned sinse he had started talking to me I would try
to get him into the habit.

He didnt anser me right off. He seemed to be
thinking. His eyes had that far off look in them. The
kind a man gets when he is recollecting something
fond. Then he said I guess its nice enough. Not fansee
but nice enough. My Grandpa built the place with his
own two hands. He left it to my Pa. When Pa passed
on he left it to me and Ma. How come your interested.

He give me a sharp look.

I allreddy told you I said. I am heading west and
looking for a good place to settle down in. I just
wondered what yours was like is all.

Three days later we come to it. Dundees homeplace
was a long log house with a fieldstone chimney on one
end. Out in front of it was a wooden bench with a
washtub on it. There was dimity curtins in the
windows and some flowers was sprouting from the sod
roof. It didnt take a sharp eye to see that the place had
been let go to seed. Chinking had fell out from
between the logs in a whole bunch of spots. The door
was open and hanging on its hinges like it was fixing
to fall to the ground any minnit. The grass had growed
up all around the house and there wasnt no Smoke
coming out the chimny. Back behind it and off a little
to one side was a barn.

I stopped next to Dundee. He was sitting his horse

and looking at the house like it was something he seen in a Vision. I wanted to ask him wasnt he going in. But I seen the mussle in his jaw jumping so I just kept my mouth tight shut.

Next thing I knowed he was out of the Saddle. But he wasnt going anyplace. He was just standing there looking hard at his homeplace. I watched him when he finally went on up to it. He put out his hand to touch the door latch. But his hand never did touch it. Not at first. It just stood there in the middle of the air halfway to the latch. Then he got a grip on the latch and he pulled the door all the way open.

He went inside and he was in there a goodly amount of time before he come out again. His arms was hanging at his sides and his face looked empty.

He turned and looked out over a field that was off to the right and had some Corn shocks standing in it.

Dundee went around the side of the house and I lost sight of him. I waited but he didnt come back. I started thinking maybe he had gone off somewhere and wasnt coming back. But that made no sense on account of his horse was still right where he left it. I dug my heels into my buckskin and walked him around the side of the house. Back behind the house was a small grove of quaking aspens.

Dundee was standing between me and them. He had his hat in his hands. His shoulders was all bunched up. I thought at first he was shaking but then I desided it must have been the light the way it came flikering through the trees when the branches moved in the breeze that had made him seem to be shaking.

There was something about him that kept me from going up to him. He put me in mind of a man who has just taken a bad beating and is trying hard to stay up on his feet. I dont know how much time went by with the two of us hardly moving. Maybe as many as Ten minnits. Then he turned around. When he seen me it was like he was seeing a stranger. At first he looked like he didnt even know me. But then his face changed and it was just like allways allmost. Still hard but not as hard as when he first turned toward me.

Shes dead he said.

Who is I asked him.

He stepped to one side. For the first time I could see the wooden Cross sticking up out the ground behind him. There was no mound which ment the Grave was an old one.

I got down off my horse and went up to where he was standing. Somebody had burned the name Rosemary Dundee into the wood of the Cross.

My Ma was hale and hearty when I went to the War he said. She made me promise to come back to her as soon as I could. Well I am here. I came back. He turned and looked down at the Grave and its Cross.

I am sorry for your trouble I told him.

He looked up at the sky. The sun was down and the clouds was filling it. You can stay the night here if you are of a mind to he said and then he headed back to the house leaving me behind.

CHAPTER 2

I went inside the house. Dundee was in there holding a lamp in his hand. It had a smokeblacked chimny on it. He slammed it down on a wooden table. It has got no oil in it he said. I looked around but couldnt find any oil. Dundee found the stub of a Candle and lit it.

The place was a mess. Dirt was all over. Spiders had spun there Webs in the corners. On the floor was rat droppings some of which I seen was fresh.

It has seen better days Dundee said.

I went and got a Broom and started in to sweeping. Dundee started in to coffing. Leave off with that for now he said. Youll likely as not cause us both to choke to death before your through.

He went and sat himself down at the table. In the light of the Candle which he had stuck to a tin plate with some melted wax he looked a little like old Lucifer himself. I will see to the horses I said and went outside. When I come back after putting the horses in the barn Dundee was still sitting where I had left him. I brought the jerky I said. I had got it out his Saddle bag. It was what was left of a skunk Dundee had shot the day before. That was what we ate for supper that night. I mean its what I ate. Dundee didnt eat anything.

He was still sitting at the table when I layed myself down on a bed in a room off the kitchen. The minnit I did I took to sneezing on account of all the dust I stirred up from the bedclothes. I lay there looking out the window at all the stars up in the sky. I kept listening for some sort of sound from Dundee out in the kitchen but he didnt make so much as a One. He could have been on the moon for all I could hear of him.

I tryed to sleep but I couldnt. I turned one way. Then the other. All the time I kept listening. After a while I give up trying to sleep and just layed there on my back watching the stars drift away from the window and other ones come to take there place.

All of a sudden there was this noise. It wasnt a holler and it wasnt a hoot. It was something in between. I sat right up in bed as wide awake as you please. I must have dozed off though I didnt know I had.

I listened. I didnt know what had made the sound that woken me. I thought might be it was an animal. I thought might be Dundee had forgot to shut the door and one had wandered in. I got out of bed and went to the door and opened it. It was dark as the Pit in the kitchen on account of the Candle was out. I couldnt see a thing.

Dundee I said.

Go back to bed he said from out the dark.

I heard something I said. It was like a howl.

Go back to bed he said.

Are you fit I asked him.

He give a grunt. I fell asleep he said. I had a Nightmare thats all he said. The same One I always have.

I put out my hands and felt my way over to a chair.

What was your Nightmare about I asked him as I sat down in the dark.

My brother he said.

I didnt know you had a brother I said.

I dont he said. Not any more I dont. He is dead. He was killed at Carricks Ford.

Where is that I asked him.

In Virginia he told me.

What happened I asked him.

It was during the War he said. The Blubellys ran right over us that day at Carricks Ford. John that was my brothers name was trying to make a stand along with about a handfull of others me included. But those Blubellys was as numerous as flys around horseshit. They was all over the god dam place. I saw it was no use trying to hold our position. I told the boys we had to make a run for it. Not me John says like the stubborn sonofabitch he was. I wont turn tail. Come on god dammit I said to him. I even grabbed him by the shoulder to try to drag him away with me. But he just wouldnt be dragged. All the time the guns were firing and men were yelling and the wounded were screaming for water or help. But John dam him stood his ground while all the other boys up and run off. A Blubelly popped up out of nowhere. He fired. I fired at the same time. When the Smoke cleared John was lieing on the ground with his guts hanging out and the Blubelly was deader than a door nail. I went crazy then. All I could think to do was get John to someplace safe. I dropped my gun and picked him up and started to run through the Smoke. John was holding his Bloody belly in both hands. He kept trying to push his guts back inside him where they belonged. It hurts I remember he said. Oh it hurts so awful bad. I kept on running as fast as ever I could. By the time I got to what seemed a safe spot and had layed John down on the ground it was all over. He was dead.

When Dundee stopped talking I said no wonder you have Nightmares.

He was a good man John was Dundee said as if he hadnt heard what I said. He was a year younger than me. We werent just brothers we were frends. I dont know can you understand that.

I can I said. I could on account of what little I knew then about Dundee made me beleeve he could be bound to a brother by more than just Blood.

In my Nightmare Dundee said John allways begs me to run faster. He tells me to take him away from the War. To some place peesefull and easy. I run as fast as my two legs can carry me. Through woods and across plains and over mountains and down into gulches and up out of them. Somehow or other I know for certain that if I can just run fast enough and far enough John wont die. He will live. But my Nightmare allways winds up the same dam way. With him dead on account of I couldnt run fast enough to save him.

Its only a dream I said trying to give Dundee some ease.

Only a dream he said right after me. Then he laughed. It wasnt a joyfull sound. Sometimes dreams he said are more real than real life itself and they can be even more hurtful than real life can be. Beleeve me when I tell you thats so.

I reckon I said.

You havent the foggiest notion of what I am talking about he said to me in a real ruff voice. Why dont you say so.

I could feel myself getting hot under the collar. What right did Dundee have to tell me I didnt know what he was talking about. I lost my Pa I said to him. My Ma to. The same as you have. The only difference between us on that Score is I didnt have no brother to lose. But I know what your talking about dam if I dont. I know how bad it hurts when you lose somebody you love.

He was quiet for a minnit and then he said I shouldnt have snapped at you like I just did.

It dont matter I told him. I know you was feeling real bad. When folk get to feeling that way there like wild critters that has got hurt. You come near them and there likely to bite you even if your just trying to help them.

Your so young he said I didnt think you would understand.

I am not so young I said. I am a month short of sixteen. But young has got nothing at all to do with it I said. What counts is that much the same as has happened to you has happened to me to. You and me are two of a kind.

What might you mean by that he asked me.

We are both orfans I told him.

He didnt say anything more for a while after that. Neither did I. The two of us just sit there in the dark letting time pass. After a while Dundee told me to go on back to bed. I went. This time I fell asleep quick. I dreamed that Dundee and me was at Carricks Ford. I had a gun. So did he. Cannons was making an awful loud noise. Men was shooting at each other and dieing like flys. Dundee and me turned those Blubellys around and sent them skampering like scared rabbits back the way they had come from. Pretty soon everything was peeseful and quiet. That was when I woken up.

I went out to the kitchen. Dundee was there. You can go wash up in the crick he told me. I went and did. When I come back he was gone. I went out back but he werent there. I found him in the barn Saddling his horse.

I asked him where was he going.

To town he said.

I asked him did he want some company.

He straightened up from tightening his Cinch and give me a squinty look. The town is west of here he said. Which is the way your headed. So you might as well ride along.

He flipped his stirrups down and led his black out the barn into the sunlight. Get a move on he called back to me over his shoulder. The morning is haff done with allreddy.

I set to Saddling my buckskin. I was feeling low on account of it had started to seem that Dundee was eeger to be shut of me. When he spoke to me about the plan I had to head west he didnt look me in the eye like he usually did. I thought about what he had said and the way he had said it all the way into town.

You hungry he asked me as we rode into town later on.

I said yes I was.

We can eat over there he said.

We left our horses tyed to the hitchrail out in front of the restaurant he had pointed out and went inside. We sat down and a man with a white Apron on took our order. I had eggs. Dundee had a steak with potatoes and Cornbread. We both had Coffee. It was

while we was finishing our second cup of Coffee that
he asked me where exaktly I was planning on going.

I dont exaktly know I told him which was the
Truth. Might be I will mosey on down to Texas and be
a Cowboy.

Cowboying is hard work he said.

I am not afraid of hard work I told him. I have
worked hard my whole life.

I know he said.

How would you know that I asked him.

I saw the calluses on your hands he ansered.

You dont miss a Trick do you I said.

I try hard not to he said and got up to go pay the
bill.

I caught up with him. I will pay my fair share I told
him. I dont need a handout from you or nobody else
neither.

He told me how much my share was and took the
money I give him and then we left the restaurant.

Outside he said so long be good. He give me a wave
and walked away. I watched him cross the street and
head for the Saloon. Well I thought that appears to be
that. Dam you Dundee I thought. Walking off on me
like we was purfekt strangers. Its been nice knowing
you I called out to him.

He stopped walking and looked back at me. Then he
turned around and come on back to where I was at.

I have no use for a wet behind the ears kid he told
me. You ought to be smart enough to see that.

I guess I got no need of a surly One time soljer
neither I told him.

Reckon you dont he said meek as you please and
then he left me standing there a second time. I stayed
where I was for a spell after he had gone inside the

Saloon. But I knew there wasnt no use me standing around and waiting on him when he had made it plain as pie I wasnt wanted. So I went to my horse and untied him from the hitchrail and climbed into the Saddle. I moved him out and walked him sort of slow down the street. I was allmost at the end of the street where it give way to prairie when I heard shouting coming from out the Saloon. I quick turned my horse and headed back the way I had come. I went through the batwings and into the Saloon and there was Dundee in the middle of the room. He had his fists up and there was a man across from him who looked like he had killing on his mind. The Bar Dog was asking Dundee and the other Fellow would they please step outside if they ment to fight on account of he didnt want no damage done. But you could see his words fell on deff ears from the way Dundee and the other Fellow was circling One another like Two rams in rut. They was about to butt heads for sure I seen.

The other Fellow it was who threw the first punch. It slid off Dundees shoulder on account of the slick as spit way he had sidstepped it. Dundee threw a punch of his own and it landed on the other Fellows jaw. He let out a roar and come at Dundee who give him Two more punches that sent him dansing backwards into a table which he fell over and broke into peeses. He let out another roar and just then Two other men come into the Saloon. The one Dundee had downed called out to them to come help him which they right away went and did.

Dundee stood his ground though. Any other man seeing Three men coming at him would have broke and run but not him. He tryed to get his back up against the wall so they couldnt surround him. But before he could do that one of the men got behind him.

What the Hell is going on that man yelled to the One who had got up off the floor.

Johnny Reb there dont know enough to get out of places where he is not wanted the man ansered.

Dundee went at him a second time. This time he landed a roundhouse right that split the mans lower lip and made it bleed real bad. The man behind Dundee pinned Dundees arms behind him. Then the man that had come in with him started in to punching Dundee just about everywhere and him helpless to protekt himself.

Three against One is not fair I yelled. But it didnt make no difference. The first man took over and give Dundee a knee between the legs. I went for him and slammed a Fist into the side of his fat head. When he backed off some I got around behind the Fellow who was still holding tight to Dundee and give him a couple of kidnee punches.

He swore and turned Dundee loose. He made a grab for me but he missed. Dundee turned on him like a mad dog and put his lights out in less time than it takes to tell about it. Then he was about to go for one of the other men when one of them snuck up behind him and hit him with a broken table leg. That stopped Dundees clock sure enough. He went down and out like an ox under a sledge in a slotterhouse.

Sinse you seem to be on Johnny Rebs side the bar dog said to me maybe you would be so kind as to drag him on out of here.

If you would have fought him fair and not Three on One I said getting mad as a Hornet he would have licked each and every One of you. The Three men just laughed at me. One of them said take that trash out of here. It stinks up the place.

I did as I was bid and found it a hard job with no help. But I was Hell bent on doing it. I haff hauled and haff carryed Dundee outside and over to where his horse still stood hitched in front of the restaurant. A man over there helped me put him over his horses withers. Then I went and got my buckskin and rode out of town trailing Dundees black with him on it.

He woken when we was haffway to his homeplace. He groaned a bit and then he said whoa. I drew rein. He slid down to the ground. He sat on it for a minnit touching his head where he had been hit with the table leg. What happened he said. Before I could say a word he said dont tell me I remember now all to well.

I will help you get into the Saddle I said.

He stood up. He was swaying and looking at me. Then he started to grin. I guess I was wrong he said.

About what I said as I got down from my horse.

About not having any use for a wet behind the ears kid. Seems like I do at that.

I remembered what I had said to him and real sheepish I said I am sorry I called you a surly One time soljer.

I am willing to let bygones be bygones if you are he said. He was still grinning at me. I said that was fine with me. Then I asked him what was it started the ruckus in the Saloon.

The Bar Dog and I was talking when that Fellow that wanted to fight me come in he said. When the Bar Dog let on that I had just got musterd out of the Confederate army the other Fellow took offense. Seems he was a dyed in the wool Union man. Well one

thing led to another as sometimes happens and finally
to a fight which is where you came in.

I said it does seem like folk wont stop fighting the
War will they.

Some folk are dam fools Dundee said. I reckon
maybe I ought to number myself among them.

How come I asked him.

I went into town to buy some things I am in need of.
I never did get around to doing that which meens I got
to go back again.

He said we could go back into town the next day. I
notised he said WE and not HE could. Him saying
that made me feel so good I allmost didnt mind not
having any thing to eat the rest of the day or the next
morning.

This time when we got to town Dundee shyed away
from the Saloon. We ate brekfast at the selfsame place
that we did the day before. Then we went to the
Livery where Dundee had it in mind to buy a plow
horse. The farrier greeted us like we was long lost
frends though he didnt know either One of us from
Adam. Then Dundee and him got down to the
Business at hand. The farrier said he had one real
strong horse for sale that was broke to the plow and
would Dundee like to see him. Dundee said he would
and the farrier said follo me. We did and he led us into
the back of the Livery where it was so dark you could
hardly see a hand in front of your face.

That be him the farrier said meening the
quarterhorse he had stalled back there. Dundee went
inside the stall and looked the horse over. When he
come back out the farrier said I can let you have him
for Fifteen dollars.

Dundee wanted to know did he have a hackamore. I

would like to take a look at your horse out in the daylight he said.

He is as sound as a dollar the farrier said.

Dundee just looked at him.

Take him out then if that is what it will take to satisfy you the farrier said. He give Dundee a hackamore. Dundee put it on the horse and led it outside where it stood blinking in the sun.

I was waiting for Dundee to look the horse over only he didnt. He just looked it straight in the face and then he told the farrier he didnt want it.

If the price is to steep for you the farrier said I can knock a dollar off it.

This animal is moon blind Dundee said. I reckon you knew that when you said you would sell him to me. I will akquire the horse flesh I need somewheres else he told the farrier and then we left the Livery.

How did you know that horse was moon blind I asked Dundee and what does moon blind meen anyhow.

Dundee said moon blind is when a horse cant see good or even at all out of one or both of his eyes. Its a sickness that comes and goes he said. Sometimes its worse than at other times. There is no way to cure it that I know of. Horse traders will try to hide the fact by showing you a horse that is moon blind in a dark place like that farrier did back there. There are Tricks to every Trade and if you live long enough you might learn them all. Like how to take a horse out into the light to make sure he can see good. Once you got him in the light you might see that One eye is bigger than the other. Or its eyeballs may have gone bluish. Or there not clear like they ought to be and the horse is moon blind.

Now that Business about being moon blind was some thing I never knew about before. I made up my mind right then and there to pay close attention to Dundee. He was without a doubt a man you could learn things from.

We went down the street and out to the edge of town where Dundee said there used to be a Wagon yard. It was still there. It was there that Dundee bought a plow horse and another teem of horses and a flatbed Wagon for them to pull.

I helped him hitch up the team and tyed our Two mounts and our new plow horse to the back of the Wagon. Then we rode back into town and stopped at the Mercantile.

The man back of the counter in the Mercantile called out well bless my soul if it isnt Dundee. Welcome home Son.

How are you Benson Dundee said to the man as they shook hands.

I sure am awful sorry about your Ma Mister Benson said.

What happened to her do you know Dundee asked him.

It was the gallopping Consumption took her off Mister Benson said. It happened last winter. She had a hard time breathing there at the end. She didnt know where you were she told folk so no one knew how to let you know of her passing.

Dundee looked out the front window at the people passing by. He run a hand over the stubble on his cheeks and chin. He said I should have wrote her more often.

Who is this Mister Benson asked and pointed at me.

His name is Jubal Bonner Dundee said.

Sprightly looking lad Mister Benson said and Dundee said I am in need of a number of things.

By the time we had loaded up our Wagon with all the things Dundee had bought it was well passed Noon. When we got back to the homeplace it was after Three.

The Two of us worked side by each putting the horses away. Then Dundee cooked us an early supper. It was tasty as could be. I couldnt hardly get used to the idea that a man could cook as good as most women and even better than some but Dundee sure could.

How is your head I asked him after I had soaked up the last of the sauce he had put on the dryed peas he cooked.

I guess I will live he ansered me. I only hope how that Fellow hit me dont turn me lamebraned.

Maybe it allreddy has I said. He give me that squinty eyed look of his. I meen I said its a little bit late in the season to be planting Corn isnt it.

He nodded and allowed how it was. But I dont run the way the world works he said. If I could have gotten here sooner I would have. Now that I am here I will just have to do the best I can which meens my Harvest when it comes will be late.

He was saying something about Corn being a good cash crop when he stopped talking and started listening. He got up from the table and took his brush gun down from the pegs on the wall where he had put it when we first come inside.

Whats wrong I asked him.

He was peering out the window and didnt anser me. Then he said company is coming and he put his gun back up on the wall.

I heard the noise of a Wagon coming. But Dundee it

appeared had heard it long before I did which showed
which One of us had the sharpest set of ears.

He opened the door and went outside. I went out
after him and just then a Wagon pulled up out front. A
fine looking young woman was driving it. She put on
the brake and said to Dundee I heard you were back.

Hello there Miss Weaver he said.

I was just in town she said. Mister Benson at the
Mercantile said he had seen you.

I would invite you to come inside Miss Weaver
Dundee said but the place is not fit at the moment. It
needs some seeing to.

Why are you being so formal with me she asked
Dundee. Why dont you call me Cordelia like you used
to do.

You were just a child when I called you that Dundee
said. Now its plain to see your a woman grown.

She blushed and her eyes drifted from Dundee to
me. You must be Jubal Bonner she said.

Yes maam I am I said.

Mister Benson said he had met you she said. I am
pleased to make your akquaintance Jubal Bonner.

My pleasure I said and ment it.

She looked back at Dundee and said Father and
some of the other people from around here saw to the
laying away of your Mother.

I was wondering who had done it he said.

Do you plan to stay on here now Miss Cordelia
asked him.

I do he ansered.

She heeved a sigh. I truly do hope things will work
out for you she said.

I take it you fear they might not he said.

You may not be aware of it she said but there has

been a great deal of trouble here on the border during the past year or so.

I am aware of it Dundee said. I dont expect to get involved in it.

Most of the men around here are very much involved in it Miss Cordelia said. There was a sharp edge to her voice. She went on to say when Jayhawkers come Thieving and Marawding where you live you have to get involved. Else they will take your livestok and perhaps your life. Ned Larkin was murdered by Jayhawkers last year. You remember Ned dont you.

I remember him Dundee said. He had a place due east of yours.

Ned caught them stealing his horses One night Miss Cordelia said. When he tryed to stop them they killed him.

Were the Ones who did the killing brought to Tryal Dundee asked.

Miss Cordelia give him a skornfull look. No she said they were not. None of them has ever been brought to Tryal. The fact is they can and do get away with Murder.

Dundee said I heard that some folk on this side of the border have gone and done there own share of troblemaking over in Kansas.

That is true Miss Cordelia said. But what else do you expekt us to do. Are we to just sit and be sheep reddy for the sheering.

I reckon not Dundee said. But I just wanted to set the record straight.

Now what do you mean by that Miss Cordelia asked him.

Only that the right hand looks to me to be about as dirty as the left hand in this situation he said.

Dundee you are an exasperating man Miss Cordelia said. You always were come to think of it.

Never ment to be he said to her cool as a kukumber.

Oh never mind Miss Cordelia said. She tossed her head and her yellow sausage curls bounsed around a bit. The point is I wanted to warn you to be wary she said.

I could have told her there was no need to warn Dundee to be wary. He was without a doubt the waryest man I ever met. Like how he had heard her Wagon coming long before I did and how he had got his gun in his hand to welcome whoever was coming with it.

I must be going Miss Cordelia said. It will soon be dark. But before I go I want you to promise me some thing.

Dundee kept quiet while he waited to hear what Miss Weaver wanted him to promise her.

I want you to promise me that you will come to call real soon she said. Will you do that Dundee.

With pleasure he said which made Miss Cordelia smile. Good day to you Dundee she said then. And to you to Jubal she said to me.

When she had gone I went back into the house. Dundee stayed outside to watch Miss Cordelia ride away. When she couldnt be seen no more he come along inside.

CHAPTER 3

The next Week went by like the wind it seemed to me.
There was a lot to do and Dundee and me we did it. I
lost count of how many Wagon loads of Manure I
hauled from the Livery in town to spread on our field
before we plowed it up for planting. Every time I
come back with a load there would be Dundee out in
the field working for all he was worth. He like to have
wore out our plow horse but work didnt faze him One
bit. It seemed like he was Hell bent on squeezing all he
could out of himself from before first light till after last
light.

I had myself one real hard time matching the way he
worked and I am no slouch where work is concerned.
But Dundee was a true wonder of the world. Like I
said we worked from before can see until after cant see
and it didnt seem to faze him but me I ended up those
first few days with more Aches and Pains than a blue
tick hound has flees. But they went away after I sort of
got into the swing of things and after that it werent so
bad.

In fact it got to be good. I got so I looked forward to
rising and getting on with the day and its Business.
Some days when there was bad wether we fixed up the
house and the barn until before long both of them
looked fit as a fiddle.

We was both as pleased as a Cat lapping creem when we seen the first green shoots pop up out of the earth.

There like a promise Dundee said as we both stood looking at them one early morning right after brekfast. A promise of good things to come.

You meen the Harvest I said and he said we will sell some of our Corn come Harvest home and save some for seed. That way we will save money by not having to spend any for seed Corn come next spring.

It gave me a good feeling to hear him talk about next spring which was a long way off. He talked like both of us would be here when spring did roll around again and I guess what got me to feeling good was that it seemed like I had at last found me a place to be permanent in. Not that I minded it when I was foot loose and fancy free. Its more like I had come around somehow or other without even knowing it to having a need to belong to someplace where I could put down roots and grow like our Corn was doing.

By the time I had to halt my hoeing that night for want of enough light to see by Dundee took a long look at me and said boy you look like the dog had you under the house.

I am next to wore out I told him and thats the truth.

Come sunup you will be fine Dundee said but that time was one of those times that I was so wore out I werent sure I would make it all the way through till sunup.

But make it I did and so did Dundee and we got through another day and more of them after that. The Corn it was knee high and we were out working the rows when Dundee all of a sudden stood up. He shaded his eyes with his hand and watched the man on a horse come riding our way.

Do you know who that is I asked him and he said its Cordelias father.

When the man drew rein at the edge of the Corn field Dundee went over to him and shook his hand. They were to far away for me to hear what they was saying but after a bit Dundee turned around and waved me over. When I got over to where he was he pointed at the man on the horse and said this here is Mr. Simon Weaver. Simon this stray I picked up goes by the name of Jubal Bonner.

Mr. Weaver put out his hand and I shook it. He said he was pleased to meet me and I told him likewise. Then he said Dundee tells me your to worthless to keep but he keeps you on here any way because your to likeable to shoot.

I give Dundee a look but he was looking at Mr. Weaver with a face that could have been cut from Stone. I couldnt think of what to say and I didnt know what to do when all of a sudden Mr. Weaver busts out laughing like a loon and then so does Dundee. When I caught on to how the Pair of them was pulling my leg I smiled.

The truth of the matter is said Mr. Weaver when he stopped laughing is that Dundee said he couldnt have accomplished all he has without your help Jubal.

I try my best to pull my weight I said.

Dundee says you pull more than your share Mr. Weaver said.

I couldnt look at Dundee.

I have just invited Dundee to come to supper tonight Mr. Weaver said. I would be pleased Jubal if you would come also if you have no previous engagements.

No sir I said I havent a one.

Mr. Weaver looked like he was going to start laughing for some reason or other again but he didnt. He did smile though.

Well then said Mr. Weaver I shall expekt you Two gentlemen at Five o clock.

When he had rode off Dundee said we had best make ourselves presentible. Which ment as it turned out we took ourselves a bath in the creek and scrubbed our hides so hard they allmost come off with a big bar of yellow soap that smelled like Tar. Then we made a bareassed run for the house where we put on clean clothes and Dundee rooted around and come up with a bottle which he practically poured over himself. When he handed it to me I asked him what was in it and he said bay rum help yourself. So I did. It didnt smell too bad but it sure was strong. I reckoned that the Weavers would be able to smell us coming from about a mile away maybe Two.

I watched Dundee run his fingers through his hair and fix it first one way and then the other and I would have bet my bottom dollar he was doing it for Miss Cordelia. I reckoned that was why he took to whissling when we rode out heading straight for the Weaver homeplace.

On the way Dundee kept looking at his shadow on the ground and whissling like he was some kind of bird. I reckon I would have done some whissling of my own had I a nice looking lady like Miss Cordelia to come calling on. Maybe I One day would I thought and just the thinking on it made me want to whissle to.

When we got to the Weaver homeplace we put our horses in the barn and Dundee went and knocked on the front door. It was opened up by Miss Cordelia herself and when she layed eyes on Dundee her face got sort of flushed. I am very glad you Two could come for supper she said with her eyes stuck on Dundee. After maybe a minnit she turned to me and said good evening Jubal how are you feeling and I told her good evening and fine.

Once inside the house I taken a look around. It was a nice place. Probably the nicest I had ever seen up to that time. There was big chairs and a table that looked like Four strong men couldnt move it. There was pictures on the walls and books on shelfs. There was curtins in every window and a rug on the floor. In the hearth a fire was burning.

I sat down in One of the chairs and it was as soft as sitting in summer Clover. Then after Miss Cordelia had sat herself down so did Dundee. How have things been going over at your place she asked him as she folded her hands in her lap. Did you plant.

Corn Dundee said. Its coming up fine. We should have a good Harvest come Autum. I notised he couldnt seem to sit still. He was as restless as the tip of a Cats tail. I think Miss Cordelia was making him a mite skittish. As for her she seemed as cool as a kukumber I will say that for her. She talked about the wether. She said it was hot but she didnt really mind because it was good for the crops. We could use some rain though she said when Dundee didnt say anything. If this dry spell goes on much longer we will have a real Drought on our hands wont we.

I reckon we will Dundee said.

Then nobody said anything for a spell which seemed to make Dundee even more skittish than he had been up until then. Miss Cordelia tryed talking about the wether some more and then she turned to me and asked me was I settled in at Dundees homeplace and I told her how I was and she told me how she hoped I wasnt working to hard and said I should be sure to wear a hat when out in the field because she said Heat prostrashun could lay man or beest low.

It was about then that Mr. Weaver come down the steps and into the parlor. He was dressed fit to kill and I forgot to put down here so was Miss Cordelia. Both of them was dressed up like as if they was going to some kind of party when all they was going to do was sit down to supper which hungry as I was I hoped would be soon.

Shall we have some Brandy Mr. Weaver said and Dundee said Brandy would suit him just fine. Mr. Weaver he poured some Brandy into Three glasses and handed One to Dundee and One to me keeping the third One for himself.

Miss Cordelia spoken to her Father.

What is it my dear he said.

Jubal she said and looked at me.

What about Jubal Mr. Weaver wanted to know.

Should you be giving the boy Brandy she said.

I have tasted Spirits before Miss Cordelia I said before anybody could say anything about me being to young to drink. What I said it wasnt true and I hoped they wouldnt guess I was lieing but I didnt want them to think I was to young to drink Brandy. Especially I didnt want Dundee to think that. So before they could say another word I lifted the Glass to my Lips and drank it dry.

Are you allright Jubal Miss Cordelia asked me when I started to coff.

I couldnt anser her because of how my Throat was on fire and Dundee was pounding me on the back.

When he stopped and the fire finally went out I said I feel fine Miss Cordelia thank you I just guess it went down the wrong way.

Mr. Weaver asked me did I want another Glassfull and I told him no thank you kindly One was my limit but the Truth of the matter was that I was afraid to take so much as another sip after what that first Glassfull had gone and done to me. Dundee though he had another One and so did Mr. Weaver.

Pretty soon Miss Cordelia ekscused herself and left the room and I could hear her making noises in the back of the house which was where I reckon the kitchen was. When she come back she had on a flowered Apron and she was carrying a big dishfull of something white which when we all sat down at the table in the room off the parlor turned out to be what she called mashed potatoes something I had never seen nor heard of before. There was sweet peas in some sort of tart sauce and biskuts hot from the Oven and roast beef so tender it melted in my mouth. Miss Cordelia asked me when my plate was as clean as a whissle did I want a second helping but wanting to be polite I said no thank you kindly. She said there is lots of food it would be a shame to let it go to waste. So I had a second helping which tasted even better than the first had. Desert was apple pie with Cheese. After supper us men went back to the parlor where Dundee had some more Brandy and I nearly fell asleep I was so full of food.

But my ears perked up when I heard Mr. Weaver ask Dundee what his trouble in town had been all about.

Your referring I take it said Dundee to the brawl at the Saloon that I was in the thick of. When Mr. Weaver said yes thats right Dundee said there was a Fellow in there who had no great fondness for former Confederate soljers. I tryed to steer clear of him but he couldnt be content it appeared until he had at me.

I hope you were not hurt Mr. Weaver said and Dundee looked at me like he was daring me to contradikt him when he ansered not a bit. Then he give me a wink with the eye on the far side of Mr. Weaver. I held my own he said. I even put a mark or Two on that Fellow that wont wipe off.

Mr. Weaver shook his head in a sad sort of way and said I dont know what the world is coming to when men will not let themselves live in peese with their neighbor which is the case here in Missouri and over in Kansas. Even my own son has raised his hand in anger in what he chooses to call the good fight. Mr. Weaver shook his head again.

Dundee said I had been meening to ask you about Marcus. How is he.

Oh he is fit enough Mr. Weaver ansered.

Right then Miss Cordelia come in from the kitchen and this time she had no Apron on. Dundee she said it was so hot in that kitchen I thought I would faint. I need some fresh air. Will you walk out with me.

Dundee quick put down his empty Glass and got up as fast as a turpentined Cat. When the Two of them had gone outside Mr. Weaver asked me if I planned to stay on with Dundee.

I said yes sir I do so long as he will have me.

He is a good man Mr. Weaver said. But I can tell the War has hardened him. Still you could do wurse than remain with Dundee. Where is your home Jubal.

With Dundee I ansered surprised at the Question.

I mean before you joined Dundee at his place Mr. Weaver explained.

I told him Kentucky and then I ansered all the other Questions he asked me about myself. I was smack in the middle of telling him how Pa dyed and left me and Ma to fend for ourselves when he held up a hand to stop me talking and said listen. Do you hear something.

I didnt and said so but then I did hear something. What I heard was the sound of riders coming. That Mr. Weaver it appeared had ears allmost as sharp as Dundee had. He got up and went to the window and peered out. The sound of horses coming got louder and then all you could hear was a nicker now and then.

He is allright praise the Lord Mr. Weaver said leaving the window and heading fast for the front door. He opened it and went outside and I followd him out to where a big bunch of men was getting out of their Saddles and Dundee and Miss Cordelia was standing smack in the middle of them all.

She left Dundee and run up to One of the men who had a Devil take the hindmost look in his eyes and threw her arms around him until he laughed and said if she didnt stop right quick he was going to expire because she was holding him so tight. She laughed to then and let him loose and said oh Marcus I am so glad your allright.

Of course I am allright he said. Didnt I tell you not to worry.

Marcus said Mr. Weaver as he joined the man and Miss Cordelia. I have been on pins and needles ever sinse you left.

I wish there was some way to stop you Two from worrying about me said the man named Marcus. But I suppose there isnt One. In any case I am home now so

I want to see smiles on both of your faces. Yours first sister.

Marcus pointed a finger at Miss Cordelia and she smiled. Then he turned to Mr. Weaver and Mr. Weaver got a smile on his face to. Come inside Son Mr. Weaver said putting his arm around Marcuses shoulder and walking with him toward the house with Miss Cordelia alongside of them. Come inside everyone he called out over his shoulder. I was about to go back inside like Mr. Weaver wanted us all to do when I notised the look on Dundees face. He was staring straight at One of the men who had ridden in and that man was staring straight at him. Then Dundee gave the man he was staring at a nod and the man he said god dam if it aint Dundee big as life and twise as sassy.

How are you Augie Dundee said. Long time no see.

I couldnt believe my eyes at first the man named Augie said as he shook Dundees hand. I never expekted to set eyes on you again. How have you been keeping.

Tolerable Dundee said. What might you be doing in this neck of the woods. I thought you come from Tennessee.

I did Augie said but when I got musterd out of the Army and went on home I couldnt take the life there anymore. I was real restless. I was like a Hop Toad never able to sit still for more than a minnit. Then I Heard there was action out here on the border so I put on my walking boots and here I am.

And you have seen some action I take it Dundee said.

Augies face lit up like a lamp. He whissled through his Teeth. Have I seen action he said. You just bet I have. I havent seen so much action sinse you and me was in the battle of Carricks Ford.

Those last Two words was hardly out of Augies Mouth when I seen Dundees face go dark like the moon had all of a sudden hid itself behind a cloud. I knew what had happened allright. He had started remembering how he had lost his brother at the battle of Carricks Ford which he had told me about that first night we had spent at the homeplace.

Augie must have notised how Dundee looked same as me because he said I guess you still miss your brother. When Dundee didnt say a word Augie said your brother fought the good fight and he dyed brave. You can take comfort from that fact.

He dyed scared and hurting Dundee said. Like a dog run over by a Wagon is how he dyed Augie and for no good reason. Dundees words come out of his Mouth the way bullets come from a gun.

You been a long time greeving Dundee Augie said. Maybe its time you let go of your greef.

Its hard Augie Dundee said. I was wondering what he ment. What was hard I was wondering when he said all those men dead and some of them not yet men but just boys. Its hard to swallow Augie at leest it is for me. If it made sense that would be One thing but as far as I can see fighting and killing makes no more sense than a Two headed rooster.

I hope you wont take no offense Augie said but I remember you as One Hell of a fighter all through the War. I reckon you must have changed some sinse then.

I am no coward Augie but I reckon your right. I have changed. After I was musterd out and while I was making my way west I did some pondering on things. When I was through pondering I had desided War made no kind of sense to me so I was through with fighting.

Thats where you and me part company then Augie said. I like fighting maybe even love it if the truths to be told. I like the eksitement of it and the way a mans Blood rises in the heat of battle. That kind of thing is like a Drug to me. I cant seem to get enough of it.

I can understand that Dundee said. I was once the selfsame way. He clapped Augie on the back and brought him over to where I was standing. He said Augie I would like you to meet Jubal Bonner my sidekick. Boy this here is Augie Lambert. Him and me was in the War back East together.

I am pleased to meet you Mr. Lambert I said.

Call me Augie he said as we shook hands.

Before either Augie or me could say anything more Miss Cordelia come out on the porch and called on us to come along inside. It was only then that I notised all the other men had allreddy gone in. The Three of us went inside then and the house was bright and noisy with everybody talking and laughing and all the lamps and even some Candles lit. Mr. Weaver took it upon himself to tell all the men there who Dundee and me was. Dundee and me spent some time shaking hands and learning the names of the other men most of whom was drinking Brandy I notised. I learned by listening to what the other men said that Augie Lambert was the boss of there bunch which included Miss Cordelias brother Marcus.

Miss Cordelia was making the rounds with the Brandy bottle in her hand. When she come to me she whispered you will get used to it. The first time a Fellow drinks hard likker he is not likely to fansee it much. I wondered how did she know it had been my first trip to the Brandy bottle.

I am afraid I failed she said to me next.

I dont think I know what you meen Miss Cordelia I told her and I really didnt know what it was she was talking about.

She said earlier I persuaded Dundee to go outside with me to stop Father from talking about the raids and the part Marcus is playing in them. It upsets Father to talk about them. But now here we are right back in the middle of that unhappy topic.

She was right. The men who rode with Augie Lambert were telling Mr. Weaver what they had done and how well it had worked. One of them said we run off some horses and stampeeded a few hundred head of Cattle belonging to that Jayhawker Miles Fanton.

That will teech him a lesson said another man. Its high time Fanton stopped riding ruff shod over peesfull Missouri Citizens.

Marcus Weaver went over to Dundee and said I didnt have a chanse to speak to you before. Its good to see you again. The Two of them shook hands and then Dundee said when I saw you last Marcus you werent but a tad. Youve grown some.

I have Marcus said. In more ways than One. I was to young to go to War the way you did but now I am right in the middle of a War that is raging right in our own back yards.

I have been hearing talk about the trouble on the border Dundee said.

Marcus Weaver wasnt as tall as Dundee nor was he as broad in the shoulder or as narrow in the hips but he had a raw boned look about him that made you think he could endure. He had blue eyes and black hair and I guess a girl would say he was handsom. He talked fast and all the time he talked he waved his hands in the air or he pounded a fist into his palm to make his points. Dundee just stood there sipping Brandy from his Glass but not saying much or giving him even so much as a grunt.

So what I am getting at Marcus said to Dundee after awhile is we could use you to help us smash those Kansas Jayhawkers before they can cause us any more greef. I could see the other men in the room taking Dundees measure when Marcus said that.

I take it as a Complement your asking me to ride with you Dundee told Marcus. But like I was telling Augie outside just now I have had me a bellyfull of fighting.

I dont beleeve it Marcus said. Ever sinse we were boys you were a fighter and a dam good One at that. Excuse my language Cordelia. What has got in to you Dundee.

I dont rightly know how to anser you on that score Dundee said. But like I said I am interested only in minding my own business and not in courting any kind of trouble.

At that point Augie come on over and he put his arm around Dundees shoulder and he said those Jayhawkers have burned crops and they have burned barns. They have stolen Missouri horses and changed the brands on them. They talk about a free state and being abolitionist but what they really are is Marawders. Was you to take to riding with us Dundee Augie kept at him you would be doing us and yourself a favor. At a time like this a man cant afford to put his own wishes ahead of the safety and well being of his neighbors.

I am as quick as the next man to lend a hand to a neighbor Dundee said real sharp but I am also a peesful man these days.

You fought for the Confederasy Marcus said. How is it that you wont fight the Jayhawkers who are working hand in Glove with Major Parkinson and the United States Army.

I allreddy told you Dundee said with fire in his eyes. I have had my fill of fighting. Then he asked who was this Major Parkinson that Marcus had mentioned.

It was Augie who ansered his Question. He said Major James Parkinson was sent to Kansas to stop the fighting on the border. Him and his right hand man Lutenant Evan Nordell and a whole bunch of there Cavalry are trying to do that by stepping on the toes of folk over here in Missouri. They dont pay much mind to what those Kansas Jayhawkers do but Parkinson has gone and declard that me and my men and others just like us are outlaws and can be shot on sight.

It seems to me Dundee said that the Major ought to have also done the same where the Jayhawkers are conserned.

What he ought to have done and what he did are horses of different colors Marcus put in.

He has a grudge against Missourians Augie said. Against anybody who sided with the Confederasy in the War and thats a fact. So he declares us outlaws and I wouldnt be the leest bit surprised was he to start offering a bounty on our heads before very long.

Mr. Weaver said I have heard just about enough of this kind of talk Gentlemen. Now I will with your permission once again express my point of view on the matter a point of view that is well known to most of you. When everybody was quiet Mr. Weaver said I know that outrages have been committed on both sides of the border by various groups of men from both Kansas and Missouri including this group to which my Son to my great sorrow belongs. I say it is time for the Bloodshed to stop. Dont you see that each new outrage leads to the next One. One side steals a horse and then the other side feels bound to steal Two horses. And so it goes with no end in sight. I love my Son Gentlemen and I do not want to see him hurt.

Father Marcus said but Mr. Weaver paid him no attention.

Or killed Mr. Weaver went right on. I appeal here and now to him and to you Augie Lambert to lay down your arms and to study War no more. It is time to turn and walk in the way of the lord. As it says in the Forty Eighth Psalm He maketh Wars to cease unto the end of the earth he breaketh the bow and cutteth the spear in sunder he burneth the chariot in the fire.

Everybody was quiet for most of a minnit after Mr. Weaver stopped talking but then Marcus said in a real soft voice Father I dont mean any disrespekt but praying or reading the Bible isnt going to get done what needs doing. We just cant lie down and let the Jayhawkers walk all over us. We are men and we must fight like men.

Miss Cordelia spoke up then. She said Marcus cant you see what your night riding is doing to Father. When you are out on a raid he doesnt sleep. He doesnt eat. He is becoming a shadow of himself. You are not blind so surely you can see what you are doing to him.

I am sorry if I upset you and Father by doing what I feel in my Heart I must do Marcus said.

Feeling sorry is not enough Miss Cordelia said in an

angry voice. You must stop what you have been doing once and for all.

Marcus turned on his sister and said dont you tell me what to do Cordelia. I have my life to live just as you have yours. I suggest that you would do well to mind your own Business.

Your safety is my Business Miss Cordelia just about yelled back at Marcus while at the same time Mr. Weaver threw his hands up in the air and said look what we have come to. Insted of loving One another we have become like dogs at each others Throats. Marcus will you not listen to me and renounse your lust for revenge.

Maybe you ought to go along with what your daddy wants Augie said to Marcus who went red in the face and said I will not be forsed to bow down before Jayhawkers.

Father and I are not asking you to do that Miss Cordelia cryed. All we are asking is that you give some thought to those who love you and do not want you to come to harm.

Do you think I do what I do for myself Marcus cryed. Well I dont. I do it for you Cordelia and for you Father. I do not want harm to come to either of you and it very well might if the Jayhawkers are allowed to continue there attaks here in Missouri.

Dundee put down his Glass and said its time the boy and me were on our way home. I thank you Cordelia and you to Simon for a delisshus dinner. I enjoyed it very much and the company likewise.

I will see you out Miss Cordelia said to him.

After I had said my thanks to Mr. Weaver and my goodbys I left the house. But as soon as I seen Dundee and Miss Cordelia with there arms rapped around each other I ducked back into the shadows. I didnt come out until they was all through kissing each other and Dundee had gone to the barn for his horse. Then I thanked Miss Cordelia for the fine dinner and she said she was real glad I could come over with Dundee.

I left her and went to the barn where Dundee was and we both got our horses and headed back to the homeplace.

CHAPTER 4

That night Dundee had him another One of his Nightmares. He let out the same kind of sound I had heard the other time he had his bad dream. This time to it was something in between a holler and a hoot. But this time I didnt get out of bed or let on in any way that I had heard and knew Dundee was back at Carricks Ford fighting the War again and trying to save his shot brothers life. Or maybe this time it wasnt the same Nightmare. Maybe all the fighting talk back at the Weavers had stirred Dundee up and set him to dreaming about bad things again. There was no way for me to know for sure except to ask him which I didnt have it in mind to do. I didnt want to embaras him.

I had almost got myself back to sleep when Dundee made the same sound again and I reckon this time he must have woken himself up because he got up out of bed and went to the door and opened it. I could see him standing there in the moonlight as still as a Statue. While I layed there a poor will whipped somewhere not far from the house. It was a sad sound the bird had made and somehow it seemed fitting seeing as how Dundee must be feeling down in the dumps on account of his Nightmare. The poor will whipped some more as dawn come and then it shut up.

I got out of bed and got dressed and put the Coffee

pot on the stove. When it was reddy I called Dundee and he come on over to the table and sat down. I give him a cup of Coffee and he said you should have put some egg shells in this Coffee. Why I asked him and he said egg shells settles the grounds. We dont have us any eggs I told him. Then we had best get some he said. We can take a ride over to the Bantrys and if they are still on there place might be we can buy some of there eggs. They keep White Leghorns or at leest they used to.

Dundee fryed up some salt pork and we ate it with some biskuts and some more Coffee. Then Dundee said Cordelia likes you. She told me so last night.

I said I could see as plain as day that she likes you to.

Cordelia and me have been friends for a long time he said.

I was on the edge of telling him it wasnt as a friend that Miss Cordelia liked him as any fool could plainly see with One eye closed but I thought better of it. Its none of your business Jubal Bonner I told myself. So stay out of it.

After brekfast we took the Wagon and drove south to where Dundee said the Bantrys had there place. When we got there a man come out the house and started smiling when he layed eyes on Dundee. He was young maybe Twenty Five or somewhere around there. He had hair near as pale as a Pearl. His face was tanned like leather which made his eyes seem like Two blue fires in his face. He was about a foot taller than me and he had hands that was as big and strong as all the rest of him was.

Dundee said howdy Asa and got down from the Saddle. After they had shook hands Dundee told him who I was and we shook hands once I was on the ground next to Dundee. Asa said to me you had best watch out boy that this old Reprobate dont teech you any of his bad habits. He is a caution Dundee is. The tails I could tell you about him would curl your hair and fry your fat.

Dont go telling any tails out of school Dundee said to Asa. You will likely ruin my reputation should you deside to do such a thing. Both men grinned and then Dundee asked Asa how his family was.

Ma dyed Asa said. It was Two year ago come this August. The Doctor who tended her never did know what was wrong with her. Not for certain he didnt. Not to long after that Pa got kicked by that old bay mare of his and killed dead as a door nail.

I am sorry to hear of your trouble Dundee told Asa.

It was a sad thing to lose them both and it being so close together made it wurse Asa said.

Then you are all alone here on the homeplace are you Dundee asked which made Asa get a big smile on his face. No I am not he told Dundee. I got married to April Denton. You might remember her from down in Horse Hollow.

Why sure I do remember April Dundee said. Who could forget the prettiest girl within a country mile of here. But what I dont understand is how such a homely Mutt such as yourself could get your loop on a looker like April.

Well sir Asa said it went like this. I camped on the trail of that filly day in and out until she finally agreed to have me. When she did I wasted not a minnit but slapped my brand on her in front of the circuit Preacher and tyed her to the snubbing post out back.

It wasnt like that at all said a sprightly young woman who appeared in the doorway. She had yellow hair and pink skin and a body that would drive even an old man out of his mind.

Howdy April Dundee said. It sure is good to see you again though I never did expect to see you here and hitched to Asa. You promised to wait for me woman.

Dundee how dare you say a thing like that April said. You know I never did promise you any such a thing.

I am only teezing you April Dundee said. But I wouldnt have minded One little bit if I had asked you and you had waited for me to come home from the War.

You flatter me April said real shy all of a sudden.

What way was it Dundee asked her.

April said she didnt understand.

You said what Asa said about courting you wasnt the way things really happened Dundee explained.

Oh that April said. It was that he kept pestering me so bad that I finally gave in to him. Dundee I had to. It was the only way in the whole wide world for me to gain some peese of mind. Besides which I allways took Pity on the Runt of the Litter. Asa glared at her until she threw her arms around his neck and give him a kiss right there in front of Dundee and me.

Now my Ma always said love makes fools out of folk and I reckon she was right as rain. I hoped when my time come it wouldnt do that to me.

Your a lucky man Asa Dundee said. Though I am not so sure I can say the same for April given the sins of your Youth which I happen to be well akquainted with.

If you dare tell Asa said to Dundee I will have to shoot you down like a broke backed dog.

Dundee held up his hands like Asa was aiming a gun at his gut and said dont fret Asa my Lips are seeled.

Come inside April said and I will make Coffee for us.

We did after Dundee told her who I was and over hot Coffee and talk about old times between the Three of them Dundee asked Asa if he still reared chickens. Asa said he did.

White Leghorns as I recollect Dundee said.

Some Plymouth Rocks to Asa said. Why do you ask.

I am in the market to buy some eggs Dundee said if you have some to spare. Maybe a chicken to now and then if you have some to sell.

I will go and gather the eggs from the Henhouse April said while you men talk. How many do you want Dundee.

Two Dozen if you can spare that many Dundee said. This boy here is eating me out of house and home.

Thats not True I said before I saw the smile on Dundees face and knew he was just funning me. Then April asked me if I wanted to help her so I went with her to the Henhouse out back.

Later on when we was fixing to leave Dundee asked how much was the eggs and Asa said no charge. But Dundee said he wanted to pay for them and finally it was April who said Ten cents the Dozen and the chicken I am going to give you to take with you is my gift to Jubal.

So thats how it went with us getting eggs cheeper than I ever heard tell of at Ten cents the Dozen.

On the way home I asked Dundee do you ever get an itch to get marryed and have Children.

He give me a sidelong look and said why do you ask.

Missus Bantry told me while we was gathering up

the eggs that she and Mister Bantry had been married for nigh on to Three years and she was happyer now than she was the day she was a bride and she was happy then. That set me to thinking. I myself dont intend to marry until I have seen a lot more of the world than I have so far. I just wondered where you stood on the matter.

When I know the anser to your Question I will let you know Dundee said.

That afternoon we went back to work on the barn which we had been working on once the planting was over and done with. I liked it in the barn. It was cool and dark even at high noon and it had a smell of horses and of leather and of hay long ago gone. We had bought some lumber at the Sawmill in town on One of our trips and we used it to fix up some holes in the floor of the Loft. There was no need to fix the ground floor seeing as how it was nothing but dirt. We put new rope in the pulley which hauled bales of hay up to the Loft and oiled it to stop it from squeeking. Dundee put some new slats in a broke feed bin and while he was doing that I gathered up some empty rotting grain Saks and some dryed out and no good anymore peeces of leather harness and threw them out.

We worked all day in the barn and the next all day out in the Corn field. By the time we stopped work to make our nooning the sweat was running off me like a river. Off Dundee to. By the time we had eat and gone back to work the big Sikamore tree at the edge of the field was alive with more Crows than I could count. They all kept kawing like they was sending us a message. The only things I could think of that made more of a racket than those black as the Pit Crows did was June bugs.

They are thanking us in advance Dundee said.

When I asked him what he ment he said those old Crows are smart. They see us out here tending to the Corn and they are just biding there time until the ears pop out and they can start in to feesting.

I helped my Ma make a Scarecrow for our field once I said. It had a wornout Sak coat on it that had belonged to Pa and One of her straw hats that had seen better days. It was a wonder.

Did it work Dundee asked me as he bent over his hoeing and sweat dripped from his face into the dirt between the rows.

It sure did I told him. Not a Crow come near our field the whole of that summer.

Then you are hereby appointed cheef Scarecrow maker for this field he said.

Next day I had a Scarecrow propped up on Two crossed sticks sitting smack in the middle of our Corn field. Its clothes werent much. I had made them out of the rotted grain sacks I had tossed out of the barn. Some of the peeces of harness I had tossed out I used for Suspenders. Its head was made of a grain Sak stuffed with straw. I had charred a peece of wood and used it to draw a face on the Sack. It had no legs but before long the Corn would be high enough so maybe the Crows wouldnt notise those missing parts.

I dont meen to make it sound like all we done was work though I admit most days was nothing but work. Still there was days or parts of them when we went into town or Dundee went calling on Miss Cordelia which he did a lot and there was other times when he said to me all work and no play makes Jack a dull boy so why dont you go find some mischuff you can get yourself into. He lent me his brush gun a time or Two

and I took it out to the woods and practised shooting at
varmints. After awhile I got so I could hit what I
aimed at Eight or Nine times out of Ten. So we had
meat on the table more often than not.

We was both out hoeing in the field One day when
we seen the soljers off in the distance. I was bent down
with my nose allmost next to the ground when I
notised that Dundee was standing straight as an arrow
in the next row. At first I hadnt notised anything on
account of how One or the other of us was allways
straightening up to get the cricks out our necks and
our backs. But when he stayed straight up for some
time I also stood straight up to see what it was he was
looking at and what he was looking at turned out to be
soljers.

They was far off but not so far you couldnt see they
was men in Uniform and not sodbusters or range
riders. They was coming our way. Dundee stood there
leaning on his Hoe like he was waiting to welcome
them but the look on his face when they drew rein at
the edge of the field werent what you could call a
welcomeing look by any manner or meens.

Did you happen to see any riders come this way the
soljer that seemed to be in charge asked us. Dundee
said he hadnt. The head soljer looked at me. I aint seen
nobody I said.

We were tracking some men said the soljer. We lost
there trail. We thought they might have come this way.

Dundee bent down and busyed himself hoeing. I
followd his lead and did the same.

You wouldnt happen to be withholding information
from duly appointed Representatives of the Federal
Government would you mister the head soljer asked
aiming his Question straight at Dundee. When

Dundee didnt say nothing the soljer said maybe I should send my men to search your house.

Dundee stopped hoeing but at first he didnt stand straight up. Then he did and he looked that soljer straight in the eyes and he said if you or any of your men so much as puts a toe over my Threshhold I will shoot him.

The soljer didnt say another word. He just up and rode off with the other soljers.

When they had gone I asked Dundee would you really shoot them if they searched the house.

I dont go around making idle threts he said and started in to hoeing again.

The next day was Sunday and Dundee said it was high time he took a look around the countryside. He asked me did I want to come with him and I said sure so the Two of us got our horses and rode out.

We had been out for about an Hour when Dundee said those soljers that was pestering us Yesterday come from Kansas. How do you know that I asked him. There are there tracks he said and pointed to some hoofprints on the ground on our side of a field that had knee high grass growing in it. Kansas is over on the other side of that field he said.

I could see that a lot of horses had been traveling together on account of the way the ground was all tore up where they had passed by. Maybe it wasnt those soljers I said to Dundee. Maybe it was just some Cowboys.

When it comes to reading sign Dundee said you have a lot to learn. Take a good gander at those tracks. There are Two tracks which show men riding side by side the way soljers do on patrol. No Cowboys made those tracks.

But you said they come from Kansas I said.

Thats right I did and they did Dundee said.

I pointed to the grass figuring this time I had got him and said the grass in that field is bent in the direction of Kansas. If the soljers had come from Kansas wouldnt the grass be bent in this direction.

No it wouldnt be Dundee said. Had men walked through the grass in that field you would be right about the way it would bend sinse men walking bend the grass in the direction they are going. But horses or cattle when they walk there hoofs swing in a circle and so they kick the grass down so that it faces in the direction they come from like in this case.

I guess your right I said. I do have a lot to learn about how to read sign.

Dundee never said I will teech you but teech me he did that day and a lot of other times when we happened to be out riding. On our way back to the homeplace he pointed and said there is water over there.

I dont see any I said.

See those Sparrows he said. Birds fly to water twice a day. Morning and evening. Its evening now and they are on there way to water. Watch.

I watched.

When the birds dropped down of sight Dundee said thats where the water is. And look over there. Do you see that trail. Thats where Critters are in the habit of making there way to the water.

Dundee taught me lots of things about reading sign. Like how to judge the weight of a rider and if there was only One on a horse by how deep a horses hoofs dug down into the ground. He told me how a man might try to hide his backtrail by riding through a

stream. But thats not such a smart thing to do he said
on account of horses hoofs go down deep in wet sand
and if your not to far behind the man riding through
the water chanses are the stream wont alltogether
wipe out traces of his trail.

I said to him you can read sign so good I bet you
could track bees through a Blizzard.

He just grinned at me.

We was on our way back to the homeplace with the
sun allmost down under the Horizun when we spotted
soljers up ahead of us and coming our way. When they
got closer to us I saw they had a man with them who
was no soljer. He was a man I knew by sight though
his name I had forgot. How I knew him was he was at
the Weaver homeplace the night Dundee and I went
there for supper. He was One of the men who rode
with Augie Lambert.

When Dundee drew rein so did I. Both of us sat our
Saddles and watched the soljers. When they was
abreast of us the soljer in charge called a halt and
walked his horse up to us. That man there he said
pointing at the man who I now could see had his hands
tyed behind his back is the kind of Missouri skum we
have been looking for. Do you know him by any
chanse.

Dundee said I met the man once.

Is he a friend of yours the soljer asked.

I told you I met him once thats all Dundee ansered.

The soljer said the men who were with him got
away from my patrol. Do you by any chance happen
to know the names of the men he was riding with.

I am not a man much given to gossip Dundee said.

Gossip said the soljer like he hadnt heard the word
right. I am not gossiping mister. This is a military

matter of Grave importance. I am charged with the duty of rounding up as many Missourians who have been raiding across the border in Kansas as I can. Now I will ask you once again. Do you know the names of the men our Prisoner had been riding with and who escaped from us earlier today.

Do you know of some law that says I got to talk to you Dundee asked.

At first the soljer didnt say anything but then he did. He said you are most certainly an insolent sonofabitch sir. What is your name.

My name is Dundee Dundee said. Whats yours.

My name is Lutenant Evan Nordell. I shall remember your name Dundee. You may well have good reason to remember mine. With that he put heels to his horse and rode away with the other soljers and there Prisoner.

When they had gone I asked Dundee what they were going to do with the man they had caught.

I dont know Dundee ansered.

Will they shoot or maybe hang him I asked.

I told you I dont know Dundee said.

I said no more sinse my Questions seemed to make Dundee mad or maybe he was mad at Lutenant Nordell. As we rode along I took to pondering what the Lutenant had said about remembering Dundees name. I couldnt figure out what he had in mind but whatever it was I figured it for far from good news.

When we got home it was allmost dark. There was a Wagon parked in front of the house. We had just swung down to the ground when Miss Cordelia come around the side of the house.

Dundee touched the brim of his hat to her and I did likewise.

I had hoped to see you both at church this morning Miss Cordelia said with her eyes on Dundee. When I didnt I rode over this evening to see if you were both allright. You are arent you.

I am Dundee told her before I could say so much as a word. But I am not much of a church going man he said and handed his reins to me. I took the hint and led our horses to the barn. When I come back him and Miss Cordelia was walking out aways from the house under a new moon that was just rising. I went inside and lit the lamp. Then I ate me a biskut which I washed down with some day old Coffee I heated up after putting some more wood on the fire. I sit there at the table watching the moon climb high in the sky and listening to the sound of a fox barking now and then not far from the house. I took to reading an old dog eared copy of a Book I had taken out my Saddle bag and brought inside with me. It was called Danger Rides the Trail and it was written by somebody named Frank Fosdick. I had started reading it long before I first run into Dundee but I hadnt had a chanse to read it much sinse that day. I was running my finger along the lines that told about an Ambush and how Five Desperadoes jumped an unarmed man down in Texas and how they beat him Bloody when it hit me that I was reading the same words over and over again.

So I closed the Book and put it down. I got up and went over to the window and looked out. The moon made the night bright but I seen no sign of Dundee and Miss Cordelia. Her Wagon was still parked in front of the house so I knew she hadnt gone on home. I had gone back to the table and sit down and was comensing to read again when the door opened and the Two of them walked in on me.

Its a nice night out Dundee said standing just inside
the door. Its a nice night to take a walk in he said and
give me a squinty look. I looked at him and then at
Miss Cordelia who looked down like she was
embarased and then it hit me right between the eyes
what Dundee wanted. I could feel my face getting hot
and probably red as I put down my Book and said
sinse its such a nice night for a walk I think I will take
me One. Without any more ado I was up and out of
the house like the Devil himself was on my backtrail. I
walked for a long time and then come on back to find
no light in the window of the house and Miss
Cordelias Wagon still there. There was nothing for it
but to go to the barn which I did on account of how I
was tired of walking. I climbed up in the Loft and lay
me down in some hay and fell fast asleep. When I
woken I climbed down and took a look at the house.
The lamp was lit again and Miss Cordelias Wagon was
gone. I went inside the house and found that Dundee
was asleep. He must have left the light on for me to see
by. I remember that night as clear as a Bell on account
of Dundee never once let out neither hoot nor holler
or any such thing the whole night long.

When Saturday rolled around Dundee anounsed to
me that come nightfal he was going to take Miss
Cordelia to a danse in town at the Masons hall. Your
welcome to tag along he told me. I asked him did he
ever hear the old saying about Two is company and
Threes a Crowd. Dont go and get your dander up he
said to me and I said back that my dander was a far
peece from up. He said you dont have to stick like a
Tick to a Hound with us at the danse. You could scout
about and maybe find yourself a filly of your own. I

thought about that for a minnit and then I said I
would come with him and Miss Cordelia which I did.

We called for her in our Wagon and when we got to
the danse and she heard the Fiddle Music coming
through the open windows of the Masons hall she
grabbed me and Dundee by the hands and praktically
dragged us both inside. The music stopped for a
minnit and then it started up again and before I knew
what was happening I was in the middle of a set which
inkluded Miss Cordelia and Dundee and some other
folk.

I pulled free of Miss Cordelia and said I dont know
the first thing about dansing. Dont fret she said just
lissen to the caller. He will tell you what to do.

The Fiddler started up again and the caller sung out
and wether I wanted to or not I was dansing. I
remember that first danse like it happened yesterday.
If I do say so myself I caught on pretty quick which
was a fairly easy thing to do on account of the way the
caller sang out like this.

> Get your little sage Hens reddy
> Balance all and do see do
> Swing your girls and run away
> Right and left and gents sasshay
> Gents to right and swing or cheat
> On to the next girl and repeat
> Balance next and dont be shy
> Swing your pard and swing her high

I got to swing Miss Cordelia then.

> Bunch the girls and circle round
> Whack your feet until they sound

> Form a basket break away
> Swing and kiss and all get gay.

I didnt kiss Miss Cordelia or any of the other ladies in our set but Dundee did. I meen he kissed Miss Cordelia as the caller went right on with

> All men left and balance all
> Lift your hoofs and let them fall
> Swing your opposites swing again
> Kiss the sage Hens if you can.

Dundee did it again. He kissed Miss Cordelia I meen.

By the time the Music was over I had started in to work up a sweat. Lets eat Miss Cordelia said and we went with her to a long table with a white cloth on it that had every kind of edible on it you could imagine and some I couldnt. There was Brandyed peaches which Miss Cordelia whispered to me that maybe I shouldnt partake of which gave us both a good laugh and there was roast beef and potato salad and pikled Beets and an Angel Food Cake. There was lots more but those were the things I had some of before we all went back to the dansing.

But before the dansing comensed a Fello with a long beard who looked to be Sixty were he a day got up to sing and sing he did with the Fiddler playing for him. I remember One sad song which went like this.

> Eyes like the Morning Star
> Cheek like a rose
> Laura was a pretty girl
> God Allmighty knows
> Weep all ye little rains
> Wail winds wail

All along along along
The Colorado Trail

I have forgot the other songs the man sang but I
remember they was all sad which put the damper on
my Spirits until I spyed a girl on the far side of the hall
with sausage curls and a big blue Ribbon in her hair.
When Miss Cordelia asked me to come and danse with
her and Dundee and some other folk I said no thank
you kindly I have to catch my breath. But the Truth
was I couldnt take my eyes off of that girl who was
looking everyplace in the room but at me.

I finally desided there was nothing for it but to go
on over and take the bull by the horns which is what I
did. I snuck in between the Crowd of dansers and
pretty soon I was standing right by her side. My name
is Jubal Bonner I said whats yours.

My name she said in a real soft voice is Louise
Stokes.

Howdy Miss Stokes I said its a real pleasure to meet
you.

Thank you she said and this time she give me a
sidelong look. I hoped she fanseed what she seen. I
tryed hard to think of what to say next but nothing
come to mind. Not until I spotted some people with
little Glasses in there hands. I seen where they had got
what they was drinking. It was something in a big
Glass bowl set on a little table and it had a big chunk
of Ice in it. What do you suppose that is I asked Louise
Stokes and she looked at me like I had just come down
from the moon and said Fruit Punch. Well I never had
heard of anything in a Glass that was called Fruit
Punch but I saw my chanse. Would you like some I
asked her and before she could say no I took her by the

arm and marched her over to the Fruit Punch. There was a dipper like from a well only made of Glass and I used it to fill up Two Glasses One of which I handed over to Louise. She drunk some and said thank you it is very good.

Do you danse said I.

I do said she.

Lets I said.

I am not finished with my Punch she said so we waited until she was and then when the Fiddler played a Waltz we dansed. I held her close but not so close she might think I was forward. She smelled of lemon verbena and laundry soap. Wheres your home I asked her over the sound of the Music. Do you live close by.

I live in town she ansered. I have never seen you in town before.

I dont live in town I told her. I am a country boy. See that big shouldered fello over there with the pretty woman on his arm. Thats Dundee. I live with him.

Is he your kin Louise wanted to know.

No he is not I said. We are just together is all. When the Music stopped I said do you want some more Fruit Punch. She said no one Glassful was quite enuff thank you. We went and stood against the wall and neither One of us said anything for awhile and then I said it sure is getting hot in here. I reckon its the Fiddlers fault. Would you like to walk out in the fresh air.

I dont mind if I do she said.

So we walked out side by side but not anywhere near to touching. The moon was up and the stars was out and as we come round the end of the building we run smack into a bunch of men with Dundee in the middle of them. One of them I seen was Augie

Lambert and he was passing a Whisky bottle from hand to hand and laughing a lot.

When Dundee spotted me he stepped away from Augie and the others and said would you be so kind as to introduce me to your lady. I wanted to tell him Louise wasnt no lady. I didnt think she was any older than me. She was just a girl. But I desided that was just Dundees way of talking with the Whisky sloshing around inside him so I just said this here is Louise Stokes. Louise this is Dundee the man I was telling you about before.

How do you do Miss Stokes Dundee said in a voice like a man might use in Church. Its an honor to meet you.

Louise said thank you and something else I couldnt catch and then she was looking at me with a scared look in her eyes on account of Dundee had her hand in his and was bending over and kissing the back of it. She looked releeved when he let go of it.

I want to tell you something about your friend Jubal he said then and knowing Dundee I held my breath. He is a fine upstanding young man and a hard worker said Dundee then. He stands by his friends when they are in trouble and I have no doubt that he will make some woman a good husband when the time comes. Dundees voice was still Church sollem. I didnt know wether he was poking fun at me or praising me. Or maybe doing a little bit of both.

I have to go back in Louise said looking like she might bolt at any minnit. Me to I said. Be seeing you Dundee.

Once back inside I told Louise that she werent to pay no mind to Dundee and his joshing ways.

Is he French she asked me.

I dont know I ansered. Why do you ask.

I read a book once about France. In it men were allways kissing ladys hands.

I thought about that for a minnit. Maybe Dundee was French or One of them other Nationalitys that did fansee things like kissing ladys hands. I was still thinking about it when I heard what sounded like shots fired outside the hall. The dansing stopped but the Fiddler kept on playing. Then there were more sounds and I knew they was shots for sure. The Fiddler stopped playing. People looked wide eyed at each other and ran to the windows and the doors. But before they got there in come Dundee and the men he had been with outside with there hands in the air. Behind them marched men I had never seen before with guns in there hands and hard looks on there faces.

CHAPTER 5

Who are they Louise said in a low voice meening who
were the men with the guns. Before I could tell her I
didnt know somebody near us whisperd Jayhawkers.
Louise let out a moan and I allmost did to when I seen
that none of the men who had been outside had there
guns on any more. Then I notised there guns was
stuck in the belts of the men somebody had said was
Jayhawkers. Dundees I seen was in the belt of the
Jayhawker who seemed to be in charge.

That man had a big black mustache and sideburns
and eyes black as coal and he was the One who said I
see you folk have been having a high old time. Well I
am here to tell you that time is now at an end. My
name is Kansas Jack Fowler and these boys with me
have come to releeve you folk of your valuables.
Everybody get back against the walls on both sides of
the room. Move fast so we can get this over with and
be on our way.

Folk started skurrying then and there was a
commoshun until everybody had his back against the
wall including the men that had been outside. Dundee
was standing next to Miss Cordelia down the line from
where Louise and me was at. She had run to him when
the commoshun started and held tight to his arm. He
leaned out and looked down the line until he spotted

me. He nodded and I nodded back to let him know I was allright and could see that he was to.

Go get them boys Kansas Jack yelled and his men went haff to One side of the room and haff to the other. They had Gunny Saks and guns in there hands. They held out the Gunny Saks and folk started putting into them there Purses and any money they had in there pockets. Men and women both put in any rings and watches they was wearing.

Louise said something but the only word I could make out on account of she spoke so low was scared.

Dont be scared I told her. They wont hurt you. I didnt know if that was true or not but I said it in the hope that it would make her feel better. But by the tight look on her face and the way her eyes kept blinking I could tell it hadnt.

All of a sudden One of Kansas Jacks men was standing in front of Louise. He had his gun in One hand and a Gunny Sak in the other. He was holding out the Sak to Louise. She said I dont have any money. I dont even have a purse. The man grinned at her. Some women he said keep there poke tucked under there garter. Do you. Louise shook her head. I dont beleeve you the man said. He shifted the Gunny Sak to his gun hand and put his free hand on Louises leg. She let out a little cry and tryed to back away from him only she couldnt on account of she was allreddy up against the wall the same as me.

My that is pure prime meat the man said with his hand roaming up and down Louises leg. I could hear her breath gush out from between her lips. I could feel my Blood boiling up in me. When Louise started to cry my Blood boiled over and I went for the man who was molesting her. I hit him One in the gut and he

grunted and dropped his Gunny Sak. I hit him
another One in the gut and aimed then for his jaw
which I missed when he jerked to One side.

I saw him swing his gun hand but I didnt move fast
enuff and I took a smart crack on the left side of my
head from his gun barel. It put me on the floor and it
sent white lights flashing before my eyes like shooting
stars. I heard the sound of the shot but it seemed to
come from a long way off. Then the white lights
turned red and my left leg felt set on fire and I knew I
had been shot. I tryed to get out of the way when I
seen the man standing over me pull back the hammer
of his gun to shoot me again.

But when I moved my leg hurt so bad I dont think I
shifted more than an inch or Two. Then something
come between me and the man with the gun. It taken
me awhile to see that the something was Dundee.
What happened next happened so fast I wasnt
alltogether sure I seen what I thought I seen which
was Dundee knocking the gun out the mans hand and
ramming a knee into his groyn and spinning him
around and wrapping One of his arms around his neck
while with his free hand he pulled a knife from out his
right Boot and put its Blade to the mans throat and
said loud enuff for the whole world to hear if any of
you Jayhawkers moves or so much as sweats this man
dies.

You tell them Dundee Augie Lambert yelled from
the other side of the room.

I had heard talk about you Jayhawkers Dundee said
with his eyes on Kansas Jack. I heard some bad talk.
But nobody ever told me you would shoot a boy who
had no Weppon with which to defend himself.

Kansas Jack took a step toward Dundee. Whats to

stop me or One of my men from taking One of your people he asked. If we did that we would have us a Mexican standoff.

Dundee didnt anser in words. Insted he run his knife Blade along his prisoners Throat and I seen the thin red line of Blood it left. I reckon Kansas Jack seen it to on account of he stepped back and told his men to head for the door.

Not so fast Dundee said. Leave your Gunny Saks and the guns you took from us behind.

When the men kept heading for the door Dundees prisoner screamed.

Kansas Jack looked back and saw how Dundee had cut off part of the ear of the man he was still holding tight to. He give an order and his men dropped there Saks and the guns they had took from the men outside.

Let him go Kansas Jack said to Dundee.

I will when you boys are out of sight Dundee said.

How do I know I can beleeve you Kansas Jack asked.

You dont Dundee said. You will just have to trust me.

Kansas Jack called Dundee a few choice names which made the ladys present go red in the face and then him and his men they left.

Get your guns Dundee yelled and the men grabbed them up off the floor. Make sure there gone Dundee yelled and some of the men who had guns went outside. Dundee let his prisoner go and then he nelt down alongside of me and cut open my Jeans where the bullet had gone through them. Is it bad I asked him but he didnt anser. What he did was pick me up in both arms and he carried me out the building and before I knew it I was laying on a table in the Doctors house and the Doctor was taking a gander at my leg

where I was hit and then sopping up some of the
Blood with some Cotten. The bullets still in there he
said to Dundee who was standing alongside the table.
Then to me he said I will take it out for you but its
going to hurt a bit. I can stand it I told him though to
tell the Truth I didnt know could I. The Doctor left
and when he come back he had a Whisky bottle in his
hand. He pored me a shot and I drunk it down. Then
he pored me another and I downed that One to. Then
he took hold of his knife. I closed my eyes and held my
breath. I felt his knife dig into me and I let out a yell
though I tryed as hard as I knew how not to.

Open your mouth I heard Dundee say. I opened my
eyes and he was thumbing a shell out his kartridge
belt. He put it between my teeth and said bite down
hard. I did. I could still feel the knife but at leest I
didnt do any more yelling. I held tight to the table
with both hands and like to have bit that bullet in
Two. Hold on the Doctor said it will not be much
longer. Then he said I got it and I opened my eyes to
see him holding up the Bloody bullet. I spit out the
bullet Dundee had give me and said if I ever run into
that jasper that put that slug in me I said getting mad
now that the wurst was over I will kill him.

The Doctor washed my leg with something from a
bottle and then he put a Bandage on it. Dundee put his
arm around me and helped me get down off the table.
He paid the Doctor and then we left the offise and
went back with me hopping along beside him to the
Masons hall where Miss Cordelia when she saw us
coming ran up and said oh Jubal are you allright.

He will live Dundee said though he will be out of
action for awhile.

Here let me help you Miss Cordelia said and

between her and Dundee I got to a chair and dropped down on it. I looked around the room and everybody was still there sorting through what was in the Gunny Saks that had been left behind to find what belonged to them.

Augie Lambert was in the back of the room and when he saw Dundee he hurryed over. Hows the boy he asked me and I told him I would live. Thats sure good news to hear he said and then to Dundee he said so now you have seen how those dirty Jayhawkers behave themselves.

Dundee just nodded.

That man would have killed Jubal Miss Cordelia said like she found it hard to beleeve.

What for did you jump him Dundee asked me. Why didnt you just hand over your money if you had any and let it go at that.

I couldnt I said. But I couldnt tell him why I did what I did. Not in front of Miss Cordelia. But Augie Lambert took Dundee aside and spoke soft to him. I guess he had seen what had happened to Louise from where he was on the other side of the room. Dundee nodded and come back and said boy I am sorry that I misjudged you. I thought you had done a foolhardy thing but now I know what you did was both brave and manly.

On account of what Dundee had just said I felt Ten feet tall and as much of a man as any other in the room. Even allmost as much of a man as Dundee himself.

Those boys arent fighting for any cause Augie said to Dundee. Its not politics that puts them in the Saddle. More often than not its plunder pure and plain like tonight. The fact that Kansas was on the Union

side and Missouri was for the Confederasy dont mean
a thing to them. They hide under the Union flag to do
there work and dirty work it is.

I knew Augie was right when I thought about what
that man had done to Louise. I looked around the
room but she was nowheres in sight which was a
dissapointment to me.

Miss Cordelia said Dundee we could take Jubal to
my place if you like. I could look after him.

Thats real nice of you to offer Miss Cordelia I said
before she could finish. But if its all the same to you I
will stay with Dundee until I heel. She looked at
Dundee and he said I will tend to him. Its better that
way. You might let him malinger whereas I sure wont.

Augie laughed. Miss Cordelia smiled.

I will be out in the field come morning I said and
Dundee leened down and whispered in my ear like
Hell you will I am giving the orders from here on in.
All you got to do is obey them and we will get along
just fine. Have you got that.

I said I had got it and he said to Miss Cordelia its
time we were taking you home.

You Two go on she said. Augie will drive me home
wont you Augie.

Glad to he said.

So Dundee bid Miss Cordelia and Augie goodnight
and then he helped me to hobble out to where our
Wagon was. On the way a man I didnt know stopped
Dundee and said that was something to see what you
did here tonight. The rest of us were like a pack of
scared jack rabbits but not you sir. You showed that
Jayhawker Kansas Jack that at leest One Missourian
has sand.

When we got to the homeplace and were about to go

to bed the both of us I brought up what had been on my mind but didnt want to speak about in front of anybody but Dundee. I thank you for what you did for me tonight I said as he was fixing to blow out the lamp. That jasper was fixing to shoot me again and I dont reckon he was aiming at my leg neither. You saved my life.

Dundee didnt say anything. He just blew out the lamp. I heard him getting into bed. Dundee I said after awhile not sure if he was asleep or not.

What he said.

I am in your debt I said. I want you to know that I know I am and that I am not somebody who doesnt know when he owes somebody. My Pa allways told me to be sure to pay my debts and I meen to pay you back when I can.

Your Pa sounds like an honorable man he said. But I guess even honorable men can sire talkative Sons.

I shut up and just layed there smiling to myself in the dark.

Next day I was up bright and early like usual but my leg was throbbing and sometimes it felt like somebody was sticking pins and needles into it. While Dundee was finishing the last of his brekfast he said maybe it is time for you to be moving on. I thought at first I didnt hear him right. But deep down I knew I had heard him right. I give him a look and said do you want me to light a shuck. He didnt say yes and he didnt say no. What he did say was I hear California is a nice place. Warm. Sunny. A body could do wurse than settling down in California folk say though I myself have never been there.

I got no hankering after California I said. Missouri suits me just fine.

There is an oshun out in California he said. All up and down the far side of the whole state. I never have seen an oshun. That would be some sight to see I expekt. He give me a quick look.

I seen the oshun plenty of times I said. In pictures I said.

Dundee got up and clapped his hat on his head. Where are you going I asked him. Into town he ansered. Wait up I said and got up and hobbled outside after him. You stay here he said. I knew there was no use arguing with him so stay I did. I spent my time trying to tidee up the house but I was never much good at womans work and by the time I was done the place didnt look a whole lot better than it did before I started in on it.

I mooned around some and then I took a chair out and sit in the sun but that didnt last long on account of I had an itch to be up and doing. But that was an itch I couldnt scratch on account of how my leg hampered me.

Thinking about my leg and cursing it for giving out on me though that was no fault of mine I had an idea. I made it out to the barn where I got a Saw which I used to cut off a lim from a haf dead apple tree. I tied some old grain Saks around One end of it and when that was done I had me a fair to middling Crutch.

Later on when Dundee come driving up I was glad to see him only I didnt let on how lonesome it had been with him gone. It had been a lot like it was for me before I run into him along the trail.

I followd him to the barn on my Crutch and helped him unhitch the teem and stall them. Just before we left the barn he reached up and took something down from the seat of the Wagon. He handed it to me saying

this is for you. I took the Six gun and Holster from
him and said is this what you went to town for. It is he
said and pulled a box of shells from out his pocket and
handed them to me. How much do I owe you I asked
him even though I was just about sure I didnt have
enuff money to pay him what was due. Never mind
about that he said. Which put me more in his debt than
ever. Sinse you dont have enuff sense to light out for
California to get away from all the trouble brewing
around here I am going to teech you how to shoot that
Weppon he said. That way maybe the next time you
Tangle with somebody like you did last night you will
have a fighting chance to come out of it without any
holes in your Hide. Come on.

I followd Dundee back behind the barn. He showed
me how to load my new gun and then he looked
around and said lets use that tree over there for a
Target. Before I try to teech you anything show me
what if anything you allreddy know about shooting.

Its not much I told him. I am not sure I can even
come within a mile of that tree. Give it a try he said.
So I raised the gun and pointed it at the tree and fired.
The gun bucked so bad I allmost lost my hold on it.
How did I do I asked Dundee.

You missed he said. He drew his own gun. Now do
like this he said. You take aim. Make sure you got your
target in your sight. Aimings important. You didnt
aim.

Sure I did I said. I aimed. Didnt you see me aim.

I saw you point your gun in the general direction of
the Target. I saw you close your eyes. I saw you pull
the trigger. You come no where near the Target. Now
lets start at the beginning. Stand like this.

I stood like Dundee was showing me how to. Now

raise your gun like this and then take aim like this he said. Make sure you use your gun sight. I copied every move he made. Thats not bad he said. Should I shoot now I asked him. No he said. Practise aiming a few times first which I did. Finally he said now try a shot but dont close your eyes and whatever you do dont pull the trigger.

I dont get you I said. First you tell me to shoot and then you turn right around and tell me not to pull the trigger. You aint making sense.

You dont want to pull the trigger he said. What you want to do is squeeze it real slow and careful. Watch how I do it.

I watched his finger and saw how he eased the trigger back nice and slow.

Let me ask you something boy he said. Did you know exaktly when your gun went off when you fired before.

I looked at him like he was crazy and he just looked back at me and said anser my Question. Sure I heard the sound of the shot I said. I am not deff.

Then you werent paying close attention to the Target and whats wurse you had your mind on pulling the trigger and not on your Target. When a man can hear exaktly when his shot goes off that mans not squeezing his trigger. He is likely to flinch when he fires and that will make him miss. You got to ease your trigger back slow while all the time keeping your mind on what your trying to hit. Thats important. Right now it dont much matter sinse your trying to hit that tree. But if it was a man with a Six shooter in his hand and he was aiming it at you it would matter a whole helluva lot wouldnt it.

Yes I said sort of sheepish. It sure would.

Go ahead he said. Shoot.

This time I took my position the way Dundee had showed me how to. I forgot about how the gun was going to make my ears ring and how it was going to buck up in the air like a horse with a bur under its tail. I kept my mind on squeezing that trigger. It seemed to take forever but at last the gun went off and dam if I didnt hit the tree. When I saw the peese of bark go flying through the air I let out a whoop of pure delight.

That was terrible Dundee said. All I could do was look at him. Didnt nothing please the man I wondered.

From now on call your shots he said. Calling shots does wonders for fixing a mans mind on the business at hand. Make beleeve the middle of the tree is a clock. Twelve is straight up and Six is straight down. Three is to the right and Nine is to the left. Now what you do is you call your shot the minnit you have fired. Like this. He raised his gun and took aim. Then he squeezed the trigger real slow and when the gun went off he yelled Five and dam if he hadnt hit right where the Five would have been had there really been a clock on that tree trunk. Now its your turn he said.

I took aim and squeezed the trigger slow. My mind was so set on squeezing that trigger that I was truly surprised when the gun went off. I was so surprised in fact that I forgot to call my shot.

Do it again was all Dundee said.

An hour or so later I was calling my shots and about haff the time I was hitting right where or near where I aimed at. I didnt dwell on the other haff of the time. My arm felt like it was reddy to fall off and my shot leg felt like it was going to give out under me but I didnt tell that to Dundee. He maybe knew though on

account of he said it was time to call it a day. Practise
he said is what counts from now on.

We walked around the barn and back to the house
reloading our guns as we went.

We spent the rest of the day fighting the Weeds in
the Corn rows and it was some tuff fight. It started to
seem to me that the minnit a mans back was turned
those Weeds sprouted like the hairs on the back of a
mad dogs neck. They grew near to as fast as the Corn
itself did. That Corn it was a wonder. It was allreddy
near as high as my shoulders which was due I reckon
to the rain we had been having the last few nights.
Between the rain and the hot sun all day that Corn
sure was thriving. So was the Weeds and we went at
them with our hoes like they was the enemy which
they was and we was fighting the battle of Jeriko
which we wasnt. We had just called it a day on account
of dusk was on the edge of turning into dark when we
heard riders coming Hell bent for elecshun it sounded
like. I saw Dundee go for his gun so I went for mine
while we waited to see what company was coming.

Turns out it was Augie Lambert and the men who
rode with him Two of which Dundee greeted by the
names of Ketch and Jesse Dean Withers. Marcus
Weaver was there all slumped down alongside his
horses neck. We soon found out that he had been shot
in the back by a soljer.

They are on our backtrail Augie told us all out of
breath and panting like a bellows in a blacksmiths
shop. They are not far off neither he said. They will be
topping that ridge over yonder any minnit now.
Marcus has lost lots of Blood Augie said. He cant ride
for even One more mile. If the soljers catch him he is

done for. Can you Two hide him while the rest of us trys to outrun those basterds.

Get Marcus down off his horse Dundee said. When the man Dundee had called Jesse Dean had Marcus propped up next to him Dundee turned to me and said is your leg hurting so bad you cant ride a horse. No I said. I can ride better than I can walk at the present moment. Then you get on board that horse and ride toward town Dundee said. Watch from cover to see when the soljers get here. Then ride back here and say you were just in town. To Jesse Dean who was propping up Marcus Weaver he said put him in my Wagon. Then hitch up my teem and drive Marcus into town where the doc can tend to him. The rest of you boys had best skeedaddle.

I layed my Crutch up against the house and climbed on to the horse Marcus Weaver had been riding. Just before I rode away toward town I heard Augie thank Dundee. Then him and his men rode off. All but the Two who was in the barn hitching the teem to the Wagon.

I rode quite aways before I drew rein under some trees on a hill and looked back at the homeplace that looked from where I was at like a little spek down there on the ground. Off to my right I could see our Wagon heading for town and the way it was bounsing and bounding along it seemed to me Marcus Weaver was likely to suffer more from broken bones than from his gun shot wound. It was too dark to see much beyond the homeplace so I didnt see Augie and his boys. As I watched Dundee got a broom out the house and swished it around the dirt patch near the door after which he set the broom up against the wall. He was standing there with his hands in his pockets when

the soljers come riding down the ridge and up to him.
I waited for a minnit or Two and then I put heels to
Marcus Weavers horse and went galloping back the
way I had come.

When I got to the homeplace the soljers was all over
like bees at a hive. Whoa there Dundee said which he
neednt have done on account of I had allreddy drew
rein. Boy how many times have I told you not to ride
your horse so hard he said. Look at him how sweaty he
is. You keep on like that and you are going to put that
horse in an early grave.

I was about to say that I wasnt the One that had
been riding the horse hard when it hit me what
Dundee was up to. He wanted to be able to account for
a sweaty horse on the homeplace. If the soljers had
found that horse in the barn they would have known
or at leest suspekted One of the men they was chasing
had been riding him on account of they would have
seen how nobody else had come riding in on him.

Where were you Dundee asked me.

With a face as straight as a poker I said in town like
he had told me to say. I looked straight at the soljer
Dundee and me had allreddy met and said how do
Lutenant Nordell.

This is Major James Parkinson Dundee told me
pointing at a soljer on a big white horse. Major this
heres my sidekick Jubal Bonner.

How do you do Bonner the Major said. Well enuff I
ansered. He asked me did I happen to see any riders on
my way here and I told him no which was the Truth.

The Major and his men are hunting some raiders
Dundee said. Seems they were causing a ruckus across
the border.

More than a ruckus the Major said. One of them

shot and allmost killed a man as they were looting merchants stores. They set fire to several buildings in town as well.

We were certain those men were headed this way Lutenant Nordell said as he gave Dundee a sharp look. But you say you saw no sign of them.

None Dundee said.

If they had come here said the Major to Lutenant Nordell there would have been tracks left by there mounts but there were none when we got here.

So thats it I thought to myself. Thats why Dundee was out here sweeping the dirt. It wasnt because he was crazy. It was so as to hide the tracks Augie and his men had left behind them. Dundee sure is fast on his feet I thought to myself remembering how when Augie had rode up and blurted out his tale of woe Dundee didnt bat an eye or ask any Questions but just took charge of things and got rid of Marcus Weaver and any sign that riders had come here.

Get down off of that horse Dundee said to me and go put him in the barn. Make sure you dry him off good. Dont never ride a horse as hard as you just did and then put him away wet.

I got my Crutch and did like I was told and by the time I got back I seen the soljers was fixing to ride on. I listened to the talk that was still going on between Dundee and the Major and the Lutenant. Major Parkinson was lamenting the fact that men from Missouri had been raiding allmost daley over in Kansas and in the next breath vowing to put a stop to there Game.

Are you also planning on putting a spoke in the wheel of the Kansas Jayhawkers Dundee asked him.

Many of those men you call Jayhawkers the Major

said sort of huffy are unoffishal representatives of the Federal Government.

Are you saying they are like your own soljers Dundee asked.

In a manner of speaking yes they are Major Parkinson said.

They are helping us put a stop to the border raiding Lutenant Nordell said.

Dundee raised an eyebrow. Do tell he said. Who then will put a stop to them.

What do you meen asked Lutenant Nordell in a snappish sort of voice that would have done credit to a Cur if Curs could talk.

We had us some Jayhawkers come visit our danse last night Dundee said. They didnt act in a military manner at all considering how they insulted the women folk and robbed and plundered to beat the band.

Would you know about military manners Lutenant Nordell asked Dundee who said plenty sinse I was once a military man myself.

Major Parkinson asked Dundee was he on the Union side.

Dundee shook his head.

Major Parkinson started rubbing his chin and studying Dundee. He said I am given to understand that there are a number of Confederate Sympathizers like yourself living over here on this side of the border.

I have no doubt there are Dundee said.

It would be helpful to us if there were at leest One among you who has the confidense of such individuals and who would be willing to relay any information conserning planned raids to my command Major

Parkinson said without once taking his eyes off Dundee.

I am not your man Dundee said. I am to busy minding my own business to have time to tattle.

I laughed. I just couldnt help it. It was the way Dundee said it that made me laugh. He said it like it was a slap in the face to Major Parkinson and Lutenant Nordell who looked like he was a pot on the boil all red in the face and stiff as a stick inside his Uniform.

You know of course Major Parkinson said to Dundee that the Federal Government has issued a General Amnesty for all former Confederate soljers.

I heard about it Dundee said.

That was a generus thing for the Government to do the Major said. Dont you agree.

Dundee didnt say wether he did or not.

It would seem to me that a man such as yourself would want to cooperate with a Government whose representatives like ourselves want only to bring peese to the border.

Still Dundee said nothing and when Major Parkinson seen how he was getting nowhere he turned to me and said what about you Bonner.

Sir I said not knowing what he ment.

You look like an alert Lad. Perhaps you could keep your eyes and ears open and

I didnt let him finish. I aint no snitch any more than Dundee is Major.

Lutenant Nordell picked that minnit to jump in with both feet. I have run into these Two twise before Major he said. Both times we were in pursoot of raiders from this side of the border. I respektfully suggest sir that you are wasting your time with them.

They gave me no cooperashun at all on either
occashun.

I see Major Parkinson said looking from Dundee to
me and then back again. So thats how the land lies. He
clucked his tongue and said well I will tell you this
Mister Dundee. I fear the United States army has no
chanse to capture these vile raiders without taking
more drastik action. It is well known to us that there
are many people here in Missouri who most willingly
and very gladly protekt them from us. Now dont get
me wrong Major Parkinson said when Dundee started
to say something. I am not accusing you or Bonner of
anything. I am just stating facts. But as I said
something drastik must be done. Something that will
teech the people on this side of the border a lesson. I
fully intend to teech them that lesson and I hope they
will learn it and learn it well. Good night gentlemen.

With that Major Parkinson and Lutenant Nordell
and the rest of the soljers rode off into the dark and
pretty soon I couldnt see them any more though I
could still hear them for awhile after they disappeared.

What do you suppose he ment about teeching us a
lesson I asked Dundee as he went back inside the
house with me limping alongside him on my Crutch.

I dont know Dundee ansered.

It dont sound to good to me I said.

Nor does it to me he said as he lit the Lamp.

CHAPTER 6

We was in town the next day after some provisions when we run into Asa Bantry and Dundee told him the chicken Missus Bantry had give us turned out to be truly tasty. Dundee had wrung its neck and give it to me to clean the very night after we had payed our call on the Bantrys to buy us some eggs.

Glad to hear it Mister Bantry said to Dundee. To me he said good day Jubal. I see your leg is out of whack. What happened. He ment I was using my Crutch. I told him how come and he let out a low whissle.

Asa you look like your pet dog just up and dyed on you Dundee said to him. Is something wrong.

You remember my second cousin Jesse Dean Withers Asa said. Well they took him.

Who took him Dundee asked and Mister Bantry said the soljers did.

I seen Jesse Dean just last night Dundee said. He was riding with Augie Lambert and Augies boys. They come by my place. How did they catch Jesse Dean.

Augie sent word to me and the Missus only this morning Mister Bantry said. It seems Augie and the others were on the run with the soljers on there tail when the horse Jesse Dean was riding put a foot in a gofur hole and fell. Jesse Dean had to shoot the critter. The soljers come on the seen about then and there was some shooting back and Fourth Augie said. The soljers cut Jesse Dean off from the rest and took him prisoner. The Missus is worryed sick about him and to tell the Truth so am I. Those soljers can be vengefull men. They have been itching to get there hands on Augie and his men and now that they have One of them the Lord alone knows what they will do with him.

Thats sure enuff bad news Dundee said. But maybe they might let him go after they try putting a scare into him.

Not likely I thought on account of how I was remembering the hard words Major Parkinson had spoke to Dundee and me the night before about taking some kind of drastik action to stop the raiding. But I didnt speak my mind. It looked like Asa Bantry had himself enough troubles without me adding to any more.

Dundee and Mister Bantry talked some more and then Asa went about his Business and so did we. When we had bought the things we needed Dundee said I think I will head over to the Saloon.

I think I will just mosey about a bit I said. What time was you planning on leaving town. When Dundee said in about an Hour I said that suits me fine I will meet you at the Wagon in an Hour. As Dundee headed for the Saloon across the street I headed for the Milliners Shop a few doors down. I went in and took off my hat and when the lady behind the counter said can I help you sir I said I hope so. I am looking for Louise Stokes. Would you happen to know where I might find her.

I do the lady said. Louise and her mother are Two of my best customers. She lives at number Five Washington Street. The lady told me where

Washington Street was at and I went out to find it.
Lucky you I thought as I walked along. But it wasnt
that I was so lucky. I had just used my head when I
seen the Milliners Shop and figured Louise just might
be One of the Shops customers and if I was right and
she was maybe the Milliner could put me on to her
which is what happened.

I found number Five Washington Street with no
trouble at all and I knocked on the door of the Stokes
house and waited. It was Louise herself who ansered
my knock. How do I said to her and she said fine how
are you and I said the same. Then the Two of us just
stood there me with my hat in my hand and her
looking like she wanted to say something until I
barged in and said I lost track of you at the danse. I
hope you werent hurt or anything like that.

No I wasnt she said thanks to you. But Mama and
Daddy and I left right after those men did. Mama was
afraid they might come back. Does your leg hurt bad.

No I said. I just use this Crutch from time to time to
help me get around easy.

Everyone is talking about what you did at the danse
she said.

I take it that folk dont have enuff to occupy there
minds if they have to talk up that little fracas.

They think it was wonderful what you did and so do
I she said. Then she asked me would I like to sit on the
porch swing.

I said I would and we sat down on the swing side by
each. I pushed off with my feet to set us swinging back
and Fourth. I enjoyed our danse together I told Louise
as the swing picked up speed.

So did I said she.

Maybe they will have another danse One of these days I said. Soon I hope.

I dont know of any that are planned she said.

Thats to bad I said. Then I said if there are no danses coming up maybe you and me could walk out together of an evening.

Maybe we could she said. Summer evenings are nice and warm and seem ment for walking out dont they.

They sure do I said. When should we.

Well whenever you like she said.

What about some day next week I said. What about next Thursday. I dont have the leest idea why I picked that day. I had planned on saying what about tomorrow night but then I desided that would seem like I was rushing things so I just blurted out next Thursday.

That was fine with Louise. She asked me would I like some lemonade and I said I would. She went inside to get it and when she come back with it she had her Mama in tow. I got to my feet and said good day as polite as I could and Louise introduced her Mama to me and me to her Mama.

I want to thank you for what you did for my daughter Missus Stokes said to me. I am sorry it ment you would be shot and have to use a Crutch.

I didnt know what to say so I drunk some lemonade which turned out to be so tart it made my eyes water.

Louise has spoken very highly of you Jubal Missus Stokes said. I am sure she is glad you came to call.

I was in town and thought I would stop by to say hello I said.

That was nice of you Missus Stokes said. Then she patted her hair and said if you children will excuse me I have work to do.

I near to choked on the lemonade I was drinking at her calling Louise and me children.

You must not drink so fast Jubal Missus Stokes said. Are you allright.

I nodded.

We shall look forward to your visit next Thursday Missus Stokes said and went back inside the house. Why was it I wondered that girls had to go and tell there Mamas everything. But I didnt say that to Louise for fear she would wonder why I might not want her mother to know about us which wasnt the case at all but she might think it was and that I had something bad in mind which I didnt. At least I didnt think kissing was bad. Kissing where I come from is just what men and women do when they are keeping company.

I handed my empty Glass to Louise and said I will be seeing you.

Yes next Thursday she said and smiled at me.

I went whissling away and when I got back to the middle of town I stopped short when I saw a soljer nailing a Notise to an upright that helped hold up the overhang at the Mercantile. There was some people standing around watching him and when he got back on his horse and rode off they moved up close so they could read the Notise he had put up. So did I. It was short but not sweet. It come right to the point and it made people gasp even the men and me as well allmost.

It said that the Federal Government had desided that the people of Jackson county was to move out. They was to take what they could of there belongings and git. It didnt say where they was to git to. They had Three days to get out in. After that the soljers would come and burn down everything in sight. Houses and crops and the like. They would shoot any Livestok left behind the Notise said. They had to do it the Notise said on account of how the Government had found out that the people in Jackson county was protekting the men who was raiding across the border into Kansas. The Notise said the Government had found out folk was hiding the raiders from the Army that was sent to find them. The Government ment to stop the raids once and for all the Notise said and how they was going to do it was by burning us all out.

Well that Notise sure did cause a commoshun. People was calling out to one another with the bad news and some of them went running this way and that like the fires had allreddy started burning. They was making a general ruckus such that it brought Dundee out the Saloon across the street along with some other men to see what all the fuss was about.

He come over when he seen me and before he could ask what was going on I pointed to the Notise and he stepped up close and read it with his hands stuck deep down in the pockets of his Jeans. When he was through reading it he turned around and started for the Wagon leaving me to follo along behind which I did. When we was on our way out of town I said now we know what Major Parkinson ment by his talk about taking drastik action I reckon.

When Dundee didnt say anything I said how do you reckon Major Parkinson found out that folk was hiding the raiders from the Army.

Dundee still didnt say a word.

It appears to me I said that you are bent on keeping your own council which is fine with me except that I would like to know what we are going to do.

You are going to hightail it to Hell out of Jackson county he said.

Which took me by surprise. No I aint I told him. I am staying put right where I am with you on the homeplace. But then I had a thought. Do you want to get shut of me I asked him.

Yes he said.

Well thats fine with me I said which was an out and out lie. I will be on my way come morning. I dont stay where I am not wanted.

Understand something Dundee said. You have to go for your own good. You read that Notise. You know whats coming down the road. Trouble is coming.

I been in trouble a lot of times allreddy I said.

Not this kind of trouble you havent been in or I miss my guess. Dundee give me a sidelong look with those peercing eyes of his and I felt like there wasnt nothing for me to do but tell him the Truth. I said I reckon I havent ever been in anywhere near the kind of trouble the army is fixing to hand out.

There will be fighting Dundee said. When theres fighting theres dying.

Where are you going to go I asked him.

He give me another One of those sidelong looks of his and this One was fit to kill. What makes you think I am going anywhere he asked me in a voice as cold as snow.

The Notise I started to say but he jumped right in and said nobody is going to run me off my land and neither are they going to burn my place. The only way they will get to put a match to it is over my dead body.

A chill went through me as I listened to what he said. It wasnt fear that made me feel cold. It was something else alltogether and at first I hadnt the leest idea of what it might be. I pondered for a spell and then it come to me. What had froze my bones when Dundee spoke his peese was the thought of him dead and lieing on the ground where he had been cut down by the soljers.

No Government and no soljer he said then is going to raise a hand against me and mine.

I thought about the Corn we was growing. Which led me straight down the street to another thought which I pownsed on like a road runner on a June bug. I put in a lot of hard work helping to grow the Corn thats in the field out at the homeplace. You will grant me that I reckon.

I never saw you shirk Dundee said but what are you getting at boy.

Sinse I worked as hard as you growing that Corn it could be said that in a way its part mine.

Dundee shot me another One of his looks.

Its your land and you bought the tools to work it with I admitted to him. But I put some sweat into it same as you did. You could say I was share cropping it couldnt you. When he didnt tell me I was barking up the wrong tree I said I feel exaktly like you do. I dont intend to turn tail and run from whats part mine and let those soljers burn down that Corn.

Boy do you know you are putting your ass on the line thinking like you are Dundee said.

Same as your set on putting your ass on the same line I said.

Your a fool he said.

If I am what are you I asked him. You said you werent turning tail neither.

Dundee didnt say anything for a minnit and I had about give up on him ansering me ever when he shook his head and said we are Two fools together it begins to look like.

There will be others like us I said. At leest thats my guess. Not everybody is going to up and run on account of a Notise. Maybe if we all stuck together we could hold off Major Parkinson and his army.

Maybe was all Dundee said to that.

Neither One of us had much to say for the rest of the way home though I for One had a lot to think about and I have no doubt so did Dundee. I thought about the hard look on Major Parkinsons face when we last met and he spouted off about his drastick action. But what bothered me even wurse was the kind of crafty look on the face of that Lutenant Nordell when Major Parkinson said what he did. Nordell looked like he was about to lick his Lips over the prospekt of what might be coming only he didnt really do it. But he looked pleasured by the thought of what was to come I swear he did. Maybe he was the One who egged the Major on to what was in the Notise we seen in town. I wouldnt have put it past him.

We come by Mister Bantrys place on the way home and we had not got far past it when Mister Bantry come a yelling out his house and waving at us to come back which we did. Is it true Mister Bantry asked Dundee and Dundee said if you mean the burning yes I am sorry to say it is true. Missus Bantry come out the house just in time to hear what Dundee said and she put her hand up to her Mouth and looked like she was going to cry for sure but she held back as best she could though she did give out with a sob that her hand couldnt hide from our hearing.

Mister Bantry cursed the army and he cursed what

he called these times of pain and woe and he said why cant they let folk be now that the War is over.

Its not Dundee said to him and I wished he didnt sound so harsh on account of Missus Bantry could hear him and she had this awful stricken look across her face. Sometimes Dundee went on I dont think it will ever be over. But that was how Dundee was. He was hard and he told the Truth even when the Truth wasnt what a person wanted to hear.

When are you leaving April asked Dundee. Which shows that she read Dundee wrong the same as I had done when I asked him much the same thing.

I am staying he told her and she said but they are going to burn everything you could be killed.

Those merciless basterds Mister Bantry said even though his wife could hear him. I would like to strangle them with my bare hands I truly would.

I felt close to the same way but what could One man do against a whole army of soljers. That there was the sticking point.

You could come with us Dundee Missus Bantry said. We are going down South to Vernon county. I got kin there.

Thats real neighborly of you April Dundee told her. But like I said I am staying.

Oh Dundee Missus Bantry said then and her voice it was something like a Wulfs howl. How can they do this to us. We have never harmed anyone. All we want to do is live in peese and raise a family.

She choked on her words and give in then to her hurting. She run crying into the house.

Mister Bantry cursed again. I got to go he said. I got no choice. April is in a family way. Shes Two months gone. I cant let anything happen to her or the Baby.

Your doing the right thing Dundee said. Take her
and go. You can start over someplace else the Two of
you.

I know Mister Bantry said as if he didnt really
beleeve it. He turned around and looked at his house.
It wasnt much to tell the Truth but I reckon it seemed
like a lot to him. I remembered Missus Bantry saying
how happy she was the last time we come by to buy
eggs. I could understand how her and her man felt. Its
a bitter thing to pull up your roots. It was for me
when I did it.

Well I wont keep you Mister Bantry said to Dundee.
I just wanted to ask you was it true.

News sure does travel fast Dundee said.

Bad news especially Mister Bantry said and then he
bid us goodby and we drove off.

All the rest of that day folk kept coming by the
homeplace to talk to Dundee about the Notise. A lot of
them it seemed to me wanted him or somebody to tell
them what to do. Some of them seemed to want him to
tell them it werent really true about the burning even
some that had seen the Notise for themselves. They
said things like I still cant beleeve it and maybe the
army is just trying to put a scare into the raiders but
they wouldnt dare burn down folks houses would
they.

Dundee heard them all out and then went and
busted all there Balloons by saying things like the
Truth might not be to a mans liking but he had best
heed it if he knows whats good for him. They done it
before when the War was on he said. General Sherman
done it after he took Atlanta and then marched to
Savannah laying waste to everything in his Path as he
went.

The folk who had come by in the hope of Comfort
went away with even longer faces than they had come
with. It wasnt that Dundee ment to be meen. It was
just that he saw no point to painting pretty Pictures
which would only deceeve folk and maybe make there
woe wurse in the end. He prodded them into getting
up and going if they was going or standing and
fighting like him and me ment to do when the time
come if that was more to there liking.

It had gone dark by the time the last of the folk had
come and gone. Dundee cooked some supper of
Fatback and beans and we had eat it and was about
reddy to go to bed when we heard the sound of a horse
coming our way fast. Dundee had his gun in his hand
as fast as Lightning and by the time I had hold of mine
he had put the lamp out and opened the front door a
crack for a peep through.

Put your gun away he said to me its only Cordelia
Weaver coming.

I put my gun back in my holster. Dundee relit the
lamp. Then Miss Cordelia come inside at a run all out
of breath and with her hair flying every which way.

Are you Two allright she said but didnt wait for an
anser so I reckon she could see we was. I had planned
to come over earlier today she said but then Jesse Dean
Withers arrived at our place and needed looking after.

I heard the army taken Jesse Dean Dundee said.

Yes they did Miss Cordelia said they were holding
him in the jail in Freemont across the border in
Kansas. But he managed to escape. He stole a horse
and came to our place. He didnt dare go to his own
home. But the damage had been done.

What damage are you talking about Dundee asked
her.

They forsed him to tell them all about Augie Lambert and each of the men who rode with him Miss Cordelia said.

That dont sound like the Jesse Dean I remember from before the War Dundee said. He was a tuff young un even then. I had him pegged as One who would grow up to be a man with the bark on.

They tortured him Miss Cordelia said in a low voice. It was a fearful thing to hear him tell about it.

I could tell she was getting all choked up. For a minnit she couldnt say anything more but then after squaring off her shoulders and blinking back a Tear or Two she said they pulled off his Boots and socks and then they tyed him to the lim of a tree so that his feet were off the ground. They built a fire under him and then they let the rope holding him up slide over the lim of the tree he was hanging from so that his feet touched the fire. They pulled him up only when he ansered the Question they had asked him. When he refused to speak again they repeated the prosess until he gave in. He told them about you Dundee.

What did he tell them about me Dundee asked.

Probably about how you helped Miss Cordelias brother escape from them I said.

Thats right Miss Cordelia said. Oh Jubal she said they know about your part in that eskapade to. Both of you are in danger now. Thats what I came to tell you as soon as I could. I just hope I am not to late.

What about Marcus Dundee asked. Is he mending.

Yes Miss Cordelia said. He is at home now. The Doctor removed the bullet from his back and he has had no Infekshun. He should be all better quite soon. She looked at me. Jubal how is your leg she asked me. I have hardly had a twinge in nigh onto a day now I told

her and thanked her for asking after me. Good she
said. Then you both will be able to travel.

We are not going anywhere I told her. We are
staying put right here.

You are what she cryed and give Dundee a sharp
look. Is that true she asked him and when he told her it
was the Truth she said werent you listening to what I
just told you. Major Parkinson knows about your roles
in helping my brother and the others. He is bound to
take action against both of you.

I reckon he will try Dundee said real soft.

So you must leave Miss Cordelia said getting so mad
she was allmost shouting. If you dont have sense enuff
to look after yourself you could at leest take steps to
protekt the boy.

Her calling me a boy was like a lash landing on me
but I held my tongue.

I tryed my best twise to run him off Dundee said.
But he wont be run off. Seems he has a mind of his
own that for stuborness would do kredit to a mule.
Your welcome to try your hand at sending him
packing Cordelia. Maybe you will have more luck with
him than I have had.

Miss Cordelia tryed to talk me into leaving with or
without Dundee. I listened to all she had to say but
when she was finished I could only tell her the Truth
which was that I wasnt leaving any more than was
Dundee. She started in on me again saying things like
Jubal you could be shot and killed and you could even
be burned to death both of which sure did send a chill
right through me but I didnt let on how her words
made me feel and when she was all done or maybe she
had just run out of breath I told her it was good of her

to show an interest in my welfare but I was sticking to my guns.

Oh you men she cryed and threw her hands up in the air. Neither One of you has the sense god gave Geese.

Dundee and I looked sort of sheepish One at the other while I was thinking to myself at leest there has been some progress sinse she now thinks of me as a man and not a boy for which I was gratefull.

What are you and your family fixing to do Dundee asked her and she said what any sensible person would do we are going to leave. She was still mad as a slapped cat I could see.

Where exaktly are you going to Dundee asked her.

To Clay county she ansered. To the town of Winston up there.

I said Miss Cordelia its none of my business but awhile back Dundee and me we met a family on the trail. They was heading east away from Clay county on account of they told us the Jayhawkers was pesky up that way and they had had enuff of the trouble those boys was causing folk in Clay county. I just thought I ought to tell you that peese of bad news which might make you deside to steer clear of Clay county.

The boy is right Dundee said and there was that dam word boy again which I could not seem to shake. Why dont you head south maybe as far as Vernon county he said. Or better yet head east till your out of the reach of any stray Jayhawkers.

Father doesnt want to go to far away Miss Cordelia said. But we do have to go somewhere as safe as possible. Father plans to come back here when things die down. It is killing him to have to leave at all. He would much rather stay and fight but there is Marcus to think of. He is wounded and might not be able to hold his own in a fight. And the army wants him. There is that matter to consider to. We are taking Jesse Dean with us to keep him from falling into Major Parkinsons hands again. Were that to happen I am not at all sure that he could keep his Sanity. As it is when he speaks of his ordeel he shudders and begins to cry. It is because he feels he has betrayed all his friends. Marcus and Father have told him over and over again that no man could have born what he went through without talking but it does not seem to make any difference. Jesse Dean is a beaten man Dundee. He is but a shadow of his former self.

Let me hear from you when you get settled up there in Clay county Dundee said. I dont want to lose track of you.

I will send you a letter as soon as we are settled Miss Cordelia promised. Then after she had bid me goodby and told me to take care of myself her and Dundee went outside. I could hear them talking low to each other and then they would be quiet for a short spell before they taken to talking again which is the way it is when a couple is sparking. Pretty soon Dundee come back in and he said things is sure in a mess theres no Two ways about that.

I never seen things turn upside down so fast I said. One minnit folk are going along minding there own Business and living their own lives and the next minnit its like a Cyklone hit them and turned everything in sight all Topsy Turvy.

We was both in our beds a little later on when Dundee cleared his Throat and said you heard how the Weavers are going up north. You heard Cordelia say they aim to take Jesse Dean with them for safe keeping.

I didnt say anything. I could tell which way the wind had started blowing again and I knew well enuff what was about to ride in on it. More stormy wether between Dundee and me.

They would gladly do the same for you he said.

I know that I said but I aint going with them I allreddy told Miss Cordelia so.

You could go and then come on back later when the fussing is finished if you had a mind to Dundee said. When I just lay there in the dark not saying a thing Dundee said I could forse you to leave here you know.

Are you going to I asked him fearfull of what he might anser.

But as it turned out I had no reason to worry on account of he said I reckon not. If I did somebody as bullheaded as you are would surely get himself in as much or more trouble as he would by staying here.

My Granny on my Pas side had a saying I said then that went better the Devil you know than the Devil you dont.

Are you meening me Dundee asked me.

My Granny had another saying that I recall I said. It was if the shoe fits wear it.

Dundee started in to laughing there in the dark and before a minnit had past by so did I.

CHAPTER 7

The next day I woken bright and early like allways
and after I had eat some brekfast while Dundee snored
on I went out to the barn to feed the horses. When I
had done that and come out the barn there were the
Wagons. They was everywhere it seemed heading
mostly to the East but some North and some South. I
didnt see One heading for Kansas which made sense
when you thought about the army over there and all
those Jayhawkers.

The Wagons was piled high with chattels of all kinds
even cages of chickens. One Wagon had a grand Piano
in it on top of which was perched a Child of Five or
Six or so and tied to it was a cow trailing along behind.
I stood watching them roll along going god knew
where and I thought some about what the folk in them
might be feeling. I reckon it was hard on them to up
and leave just like that and not know what the world
had lieing in wait for you. If the army could come and
tell you to git and then burn down your house why
just about anything at all could be lieing ahead of you
and that was in a way a fearsum thought.

Dundee come out the door then all Yawns and
Stretches and Blinks in the light of the rising sun. I
went over to him and said lots of folk is on the move
allreddy.

So it appears he said in between Yawns.

It dont appear though that the lord is helping them along there way like he did when the Israelites took off from egypt. It appears that they are on there own this time. Same as us I thought but didnt say out loud.

The Lord helps those who help themselves Dundee said and then he said I didnt know you were a Bible reading Fello. You sure are full of surprises.

I dont read the Bible I said. I dont even own One. But my Ma had One and she used to read me to sleep from it when I was a boy and some of them storys I can remember to this very day. Was what you said from out the Bible to.

Dundee looked puzzled so I said you said the Lord helps them as helps themselves. I asked you was that saying from out the Bible like the story about the flyte from egypt.

Dammed if I know Dundee said. He give me a look and said wheres your Crutch. I dont have need of it no more I told him.

I will go see to the stock he said and I said theres no need to I allreddy done it. He give a grunt at that news and said I told Cordelia I would come by the Weaver place this morning to help them get reddy to move on. But sinse then I have had some Second thoughts on that Score. I waited for him to explane what he ment. He said considering the way things are around here these days I think I would do well to stay right here to keep an eye on the place. Now if I were to do that it would meen I was going back on a promise I made and for me a promise made has allways ment a promise kept. So what I was wondering he said is I was wondering would you be willing to take my place and lend the Weavers a hand with the chores that they have got facing them.

I could stay here and guard the place while you go to the Weavers I said.

I reckon thats true enuff Dundee said but I would like it a whole lot better were I here on the spot should trouble start.

You sound like you dont think I could handle any trouble that might pop up I said but I could. You yourself taught me how to shoot.

If you dont want to ride over to the Weavers just say so Dundee said and I could tell by the sound of his voice that our talk was at an end. It was up to me now to either go or stay and be done with it. I will go I said if your sure you wont need me here.

I would feel better if the both of us were on hand here Dundee said but a promise is a promise. I shouldnt have made it last night. I reckon I wasnt thinking clear. Its easy to forget that things arent any longer the way they once was.

Espeshally out in the moonlight with a member of the Fair Sex I said.

I expekted Dundee to jump down my Throat at those words of mine but all he did was grin and bear it. I will go get my horse I said and did. While I was getting him reddy to ride I thought about what Dundee had said and felt good that he had said he would have been glad could I stay here with him. Being that he was not a man who let on that he ever needed anything I figured that was as close as he could come to saying plain that he needed me to help him protekt the homeplace. I remember I was smiling when I come out the barn leading my horse. But then another thought crossed my mind and I quit smiling. I went over to Dundee and said are you sure your not sending me to the Weavers so Miss Cordelia and maybe her Pa to can have another crak at trying to get me to leave before the burning starts.

Dundee spit on the ground and then said if thats what I had in mind thats what I would have said. I am not a deeveus man as you ought to know by now.

I forsed myself to tell Dundee I was sorry for saying what I did.

He said the suns getting high in the sky. Its time you were riding out.

I got on my horse and left and when I got to the Weaver place Miss Cordelia and her Pa was toting things out the house and putting them into a Wagon. They waved to me and when I got close Mr. Weaver said your looking none the wurse for wear what brings you here.

Dundee desided to stay to home and guard the place I ansered so he sent me here to take his place. I am here to help you folk get reddy to leave.

Thats very good of you Jubal Miss Cordelia said but I could see she was down in the dumps on account of it was me had come and not Dundee. Maybe I should go inside I said and pay my respekts to your brother and to Jesse Dean Withers I said.

They arent here Miss Cordelia said. They are both hiding out in a cave in the woods back of the house.

Are you afraid the soljers might come hunting them I said.

Yes Miss Cordelia said thats right we are. We hear the army has been skouring the Countryside looking for Augie and his men my brother and Jesse Dean among them. So we hid them until we are reddy to leave at which time they will leave with us.

That brings up something thats been on my mind of late Mr. Weaver said looking at me. Whats that I asked him and he said when my daughter returned from your place last night she told me that Dundee does not intend to leave and that you are of a similar mind is that so. Yes sir thats so I said and Mr. Weaver said do you really think that course of action is wise. I said it may not be wise but it is something both Dundee and me feel we got to do. I understand how you both feel Mr. Weaver said and in many ways what you are doing is admirable. But on the other hand it might be a foolish move under the sircumstanses. Have you considered that possibility Jubal.

Yes sir I ansered and let it go at that.

I admire your gumshun Jubal Mr. Weaver said. Were I carrying around a few less Years than I am I might just be doing the very thing you Two are. But when a man gets old Jubal the spunk goes out of him. Its a sad but True thing. Well lets be about our business. Jubal would you help me carry out some Books of mine.

I would be glad to sir I said and went inside the house with Mr. Weaver who took me to a room where there was a lot of Books sitting on shelfs. I cant take them all Mr. Weaver said shaking his head from side to side. There just isnt enuff room. He took a Book down from a shelf and held it like it was a treasure he had in his hands. He opened it and turned some pages.

Then he took down some more Books and put them in a pile on the table. Before long the table was covered with Books. I started to pick some of them up to cart them out to the Wagon when Mr. Weaver said hold on please I cannot take them all though I would dearly love to. He went through them and picked out the Ones he wanted to take which he handed to me setting aside the others with One sigh after another. What kind of men would burn Books he said like he

was talking to himself. Then he looked around the
room which had pictures on the walls and a rug on the
floor and was filled with chairs and tables and things
made out of glass to hold Candles. But there are such
men he said still talking to himself. Men who would
rather burn than build.

I took the Books he give me out to the Wagon and
Miss Cordelia showed me where to stack them. I made
Six trips with my arms full of Books and then I told
Miss Cordelia there didnt seem to be any more room
for them in the part of the Wagon where she had told
me to put them. She said help me take this table out of
the Wagon will you Jubal. I was busy helping her
rassle the table down to the ground when Mr. Weaver
come out the house. When he saw what we was doing
he said Cordelia no. Yes Father she said. Books are
more important than tables.

By the time the Wagon was loaded One whole end of
it was chock full of Books and there were Two chairs
on the ground beside the table all of which Mr. Weaver
and me carryed back inside the house.

We have another Wagon out back which is allreddy
loaded Mr. Weaver said when we come back out.
Marcus will drive that One.

This One said Miss Cordelia is not able to take
another thing. Is there no room for my Morris Chair
asked Mr. Weaver. Then he said oh bother my Morris
Chair. I can sit on a crakker box if I have to.

Jubal would you do us a favor Miss Cordelia asked
me. Sure I would I said and she told me how to find
the Cave back in the woods where her brother and
Jesse Dean Withers was hiding. Go there and tell them
we are reddy to leave will you she said. I went. When I
got there I was met with Two guns aiming straight at

me out the dark just inside the Cave but when they
seen who I was they put the guns away and Marcus
Weaver said I am sure surprised to see you here Jubal.
I told him how I had been helping load the Wagon.

Its time to leave is it he said and I told him it was
and that I had been sent to fetch him and Mister
Withers. The Three of us started on our way back to
the house. It was slow going on account of Mister
Withers couldnt walk to good. He didnt say why he
couldnt and I didnt say I knew why he couldnt. We
was allmost out the woods when we spotted soljers.

It was Major Parkinson and Lutenant Nordell and
some of there men milling about by the Wagon out in
front of the house. All of them was in the Saddle so I
figured they didnt plan on staying long. But then
Lutenant Nordell said something we was to far away
to hear and Two men got down off of there horses and
went inside the house though Mister Weaver tryed to
stop them by standing in there way. All he got for his
trouble was knocked down to the ground. Marcus
Weaver beside me cursed a Blue Streek under his
breath.

It seemed a long time before the soljers come back
outside and rode off. Us Three come out the woods
and went down to where Mister Weaver was dusting
himself off.

We saw the soljers Marcus Weaver said. Are you
allright Father.

Yes said Mr. Weaver. They searched the house
looking for you dam there eyes.

Marcus Weaver helped Jesse Dean Withers up on the
Wagon seat and then old Mister Weaver climbed up
alongside of him and Marcus Weaver went around the
side of the house for the other Wagon and Miss

Cordelia come over to me and said I have bad news for you Jubal. What is it I asked her. When those soljers were here I heard One of them say that before the day was done Major Parkinson ment to go after Dundee because Major Parkinson had declared Dundee a renagade for having helped Marcus and the others when the army was chasing them. I dont know wether you know it or not but Confederate soljers beleeved by the army to be in any way connekted to men like my brother and Augie Lambert can be dezignated renagades which has now happened in the case of Dundee. You must hurry and tell him so.

I will Miss Cordelia I said. But what exaktly does being a renagade meen.

She didnt anser me at first and then she said it meens that such Confederate soljers are no longer protekted by the General Amnesty given them by the Federal Government.

And what exaktly does that meen I asked her.

Once again she didnt blurt out her anser. When it finally did come it was said like a death sentance which in a way it was. She said it meens that such renagades may be shot and killed on sight. She put her hands on my shoulders and looked into my eyes and she said you are the only One who can save him now. You have got to find a way to make him leave here until the soljers have all gone. Jubal I want you to promise me you will do that by any meens you can. I ask you to do it because I know that you love Dundee in your own way as much as I do in mine.

I looked down and said you know how Dundee is Miss Cordelia. Aint nothing or nobody going to make that man budge if he dont want to budge.

But you must try Jubal she said. For his sake and for ours to.

I will try Miss Cordelia I said.

Hurry Jubal she said. From what I heard those soljers say they will be at the homeplace before the day is out. She leaned close and give me a hug and then a kiss. God speed Jubal she said. I didnt stay even long enuff to see the Two Weaver Wagons pull out but run to my horse and got into the Saddle and rode fast back to the homeplace.

When I got there I put my horse in the barn and come out but Dundee wasnt nowhere to be seen and my Heart about dropped out of me when I wondered was I to late and they had allreddy took him. But I seen no sign that any soljers had been there so I felt a little less fearfull. All of a sudden I heard whissling and Dundee stood up among the Corn stocks and give me a wave.

I went over to him and he said how did things go over to the Weavers and I said they went fine. He seemed to be waiting for me to say more and then it hit me what it was he really wanted to know so I said she has gone along with her Pa and brother and Mister Jesse Dean Withers. He started in to asking after all of them and I told him they all looked fine to me though Mr. Withers still couldnt walk so good but never mind about them I said I have bad news to pass along to you.

His eyes got like slits and he said tell it to me.

I said Major Parkinson and Lutenant Nordell and the rest of the soljers come by the Weavers while they was making reddy to leave. Me and Marcus Weaver and Mister Withers hid in some woods and when the soljers went we come out and Miss Cordelia told me

the soljers had said something about they was coming
here today some time to take you.

What the hell do they want with me Dundee said
sounding mad as a Hornet.

They have named you a renagade on account of how
you helped Augie Lambert and his boys get away from
them. I reckon you know what you being a renagade
meens I said. Dundee didnt show a sign he had heard
me or that he knew or he didnt know what him being
a renagade ment. Your no longer protekted by the
General Amnesty the Government give to the men
who sided with the Confederasy I told him. When he
still didnt say nothing I got mad for some reason and
told him that meens the soljers got a right to shoot you
on sight like you was a Wulf they was tracking down.

I never ment to get caught up in the middle of all
this he said real wishfull like as if he wanted to be a
Hundred miles from where he was at. But I couldnt
not do a favor for some friends he said. Then like as if
he had just woken up he said those soljers will be
looking for you the same as me.

What are we going to do I asked him.

He thought about that for a minnit his eyes
sweeping every which way. Then he said it may be I
can talk some sense into Parkinson.

That dont sound to me like the thing to try to do I
said blunt as a Bear. I dont reckon there is a Soul on
Earth could do that. Not with that Lutenant Nordell
egging Major Parkinson on.

Its worth a try Dundee said.

While your talking I said they might start shooting
and where will that leave you.

When I was in the army he said us soljers lots of
times found ourselves with time on our hands. So we

would play Cards. I did my share of gambling during the War and from all those games of Poker and the like I learned to bluff and to call other mens bluffs. Maybe I can call the Majors bluff when he gets here.

If hes bluffing I said but maybe hes not.

Thats True Dundee said. There was another thing I learned from playing Cards. I learned to hedge my bets. Which I plan on doing if and when those soljers show up here.

What are you fixing to do I asked him.

Its not what I am fixing to do he said but what you are fixing to do.

Which is what I asked him.

You get inside the house at the edge of that open window there. Then if things get out of hand between me and Parkinson I will tell him where you are and that you will shoot him dead if he trys to take me. At the same time I will have my own gun in hand and between the Two of us we can down at leest Two or maybe more of them. But I am betting that they wont want that to happen so they will back off. Are you game for it.

Yes I said I am game for it.

He raised a hand and said not so fast. Give the matter some thought. This isnt your fight you know any more than its mine. You can wash your hands of it. Besides like I said before they will be hunting you as well as me. You could light a shuck and not risk getting any Holes in your Hide. I want you to know that if you do I wont think bad about you.

I allreddy said I was game for it I told Dundee and he said fine and then he said I reckon your belly figures your Throat is cut what with all the work you have done so far today over at the Weavers with nothing to eat. Or did they feed you at the Weavers.

No they didnt I said and Dundee said then go on inside and get yourself some vittles while I stand guard out here.

I went into the house and made myself something to eat but I was so skittish doing it that I have now clean forgot whatever it was I fixed for myself. What I do remember and whats most important is that when I come back outside I checked my gun to make sure it was loaded which it was and then Dundee went inside. When he come back out both of us sit ourselfs down on a bench next the house where we didnt do much talking while we waited for to see would the soljers come riding up on us.

It was near to suppertime when they finally come. Skoot Dundee said to me and I skooted inside and got down on One nee at the edge of the open window and watched them come. Pretty soon they was milling about and I seen they had Two men who wasnt soljers with them. One of the men I had seen before the night Augie Lambert and his boys come riding in. That man had been riding with Augie that night. The other man I never seen before. Both of them had there hands tyed behind there backs and on account of that you could see they sat unsteddy in there Saddles.

Dundee didnt put so much as a finger on his gun. He just stood there as easy as you please with his hands stuck into the back pockets of his Jeans and his hat tilted back on his head. I held my breath.

As you can see Major Parkinson said we have been rounding up raiders. These Two are all we have gotten our hands on so far but we expekt our luck to change soon.

Meening you plan on taking me Prisoner is that it
Dundee said.

I didnt say that Major Parkinson said.

Then you dont have it in mind to take me Prisoner
Dundee said.

I didnt say that either Major Parkinson said and
Lutenant Nordell looked Grim. I have come to talk to
you about a matter we have gone into before Major
Parkinson said and Lutenant Nordell said we know
now that you have been aiding and abetting the
raiders.

I know something to Dundee said. I know the
cowardly way you did for Jesse Dean Withers.

Oh yes Jesse Dean Withers said Major Parkinson.
He was a Founten of information. It was Jesse Dean
who told us about the roll you and Bonner played in
helping him and the rest of the Lambert gang escape
the night we were pursooing them. I had taken you for
a man of Honor Dundee but you lyed to me that night.
You said you had seen no sign of the raiders.

Dundee didnt deny it.

Major Parkinson clucked his Tongue against the
roof of his Mouth. That is no way for us to try to get
on together he said. But I am not a man to hold a
grudge which is why I have come here today. You may
recall Dundee that the last time we met I asked you if
you were interested in working as shall we say a scout
for the Army. One who would keep tabs on the
aktivitys of certain persons. Do you remember that.

I remember Dundee said. I also remember that I
told you I wanted no part of your dirty little War and
that I was to busy minding my own Business to have
time to tattle.

Dam you Dundee said Lutenant Nordell. You have

conspired with the Enemy and you dare to stand there and defy the Major now.

Major Parkinson held up a hand and he give a little nod to Lutenant Nordell. I have put out an order he said conserning you Dundee.

I heard about how you have seen to it that I am no longer covered by the General Amnesty Dundee said.

As a renagade Lutenant Nordell said I or any other army man has the perfekt right to shoot you down like a dog.

I seen Lutenant Nordell go for his gun but before he could so much as touch it Dundees gun was out and aimed straight at the Lutenant.

Major Parkinson said something soft to the Lutenant which I couldnt catch and then to Dundee he said with a smile do you really think you could live through a shoot out with all of us.

No I dont Dundee said. But I do think I could take One or Two of you with me on my way down. Maybe even yourself Major.

That made the Majors Lips shape up into a thin line and you could hear the air puffing loud out his nose.

If you meen to take me Major Dundee said you had best be about it unless you dont want to risk losing your own life and maybe Nordells as well into the bargain. What do you say.

I say you are an insolent sonofabitch Dundee Major Parkinson said. I come here in good faith but

Dundee didnt let Major Parkinson finish what he had been fixing to say. Insted he jumped in with you have the gall to talk to me about good faith Major when you did what you did to Jesse Dean.

That was a matter that had to be handled in that

way sinse the man would not talk of his own free will Major Parkinson said.

As far as I am conserned Dundee said you can take your good faith and wad it up and use it to wipe your ass with which is all its good for in my book.

I dammed Dundee then Six ways to Sunday. Why did he have to go and egg Major Parkinson on I wondered. He was making the man mad and I was expekting the shooting to start at any minnit. I got a good grip on my gun with both my hands and got reddy to swing the barel up and out the open window.

Get off my home ground Dundee said then.

Major Lutenant Nordell said but he got no more words out on account of how Dundee yelled GIT and after a minnit of staring each other down Dundee won when the soljers got.

I slumped down on the dirt floor inside the house and leened back against the wall. There was a breeze coming through a chink in the wall and it was real kool on my neck I recollect. Dundee come inside and shut the door.

How come you didnt stay out there and let them take a few pot shots at you I asked him. You sure was daring them to like some dam fool who has turned simple all of a sudden.

Mind your Mouth boy he said to me. I come in on account of once they get out of range of my sidearm they can pop off at me with there Rifles.

Dammit Dundee I said you was allmost begging them to start shooting at you. What for did you go and act like that.

I told you he said. I was bent on calling the Majors bluff and by god I did didnt I. I take it you were worryed about me.

I was not I said.

Then it was yourself you were worryed about.

No I yelled at him I wasnt not at all.

Then you were afraid you wouldnt be able to squeeze the trigger if and when the time come to do so.

No I yelled even louder only he had hit the bulls eye twise. I had been scared to death One of those soljers would get jumpy and shoot Dundee to death and I had been scared that I wouldnt be able to shoot Major Parkinson if it come down to me having to do that to save Dundee. It was the Second thing that had me most upset on account of Dundee had saved my life once and I wasnt so sure that I could have tryed to save his life in the face of all those soljers guns. I had never killed a man and didnt never want to neither which give me a sick feeling down deep in the Pit of my stomach like I had been on the edge of letting Dundee down or even wurse letting him die on account of I couldnt do my part to save him. I just sit there on the floor feeling sick for a minnit or Two and then a thought come into my mind and I looked up at Dundee who was peering out through the window to see was the soljers gone and I asked him how come you didnt tell Major Parkinson I was in here drawing a beed on him and getting reddy to pop him if he went for you.

I forgot Dundee said.

Your a liar I said. You wouldnt forget a thing like that. Would he have forgot I asked myself. No I ansered myself he wouldnt have.

Before I could finish thinking Dundee said I changed my plan. I desided there was no use dragging you into the matter. Your in enuff hot water as it is with the army. I am going to make some Coffee do you want some.

Might as well I said. My Throats parched.

Comes of being scared of dying Dundee said as he went for the pot.

I wasnt I said.

Neither was I Dundee said and give me a look and I reckon both of us knew we was lieing to each other.

CHAPTER 8

The next day dragged its feet. It seemed like it never
ment to end. Dundee walked around like a Cougar
stocking its pray and me I was as skittish as a green
bronc. We both knew what it was that had set our
teeth on edge and it wasnt each other. It was the time
passing and moving on to the third day which was the
One by which everybody in the county was supposed
to be out on and on there way somewheres else.

I had to make more than my usual number of trips
to the bushes and the third time I set out happened to
be at a time Dundee did to and he yelled at me where
do you think your going like he had caught me in the
act of committing some kind of Crime. To releeve
myself I said. Did you think I was going to Kansas.
You meen to walk off and leave the place open to
anybody who wants to put a match to it he snapped at
me. Wait your turn he said. I went back to the house
and did just that with my Bladder fit to burst by the
time Dundee come back and said now its your turn.

I put in some time making a clean bandage for my
leg out of some Muslin I found in the house. I did
some weeding in the Corn rows but I found it brought
me close to having fits bending down below the tops of
the Corn stocks and not able to see was any soljers
coming our way so I give up on that before very long.
Dundee took his knife out his Boot and sit by the door

whittling and whissling low. He had his brush gun leaning against the outside wall of the house like that was the way he allways had it which it wasnt.

I took to going round about the house first One way then the other. I must have gone round that house a Hundred times maybe more. Then the sun set and the shadows moved in and pretty soon it was night and we was inside with a good fire going on account of nights was still cool though it was spring and nearing summer.

Before we eat Dundee took off his shirt and washed himself. I had seen him stripped before so I had seen the Scars on his back and chest but I had never spoke of them. What happened to leave you them I asked him that time and he quick put back on his shirt. He ansered me saying the One on my back is a bite from a horse who never did become a frend of mine and the One on my chest a bullet did that to me.

Was it in the War you got shot I asked him and he said no. Just no was all. He didnt say who had done it or when and I desided against asking him about it again.

We drunk some more Coffee though I for One didnt really want none but it was something to do to pass the time. From time to time Dundee got up and peered out the window. Then he would sit back down but he couldnt keep himself down so up he would get again and go to the window or to stir up the fire or put another log on. Things went on that way for a spell and then he said we will have to take turns sleeping. Thats allright with me I told him. I asked him did he think we was in for trouble before the night was over and done with. Dont know he said but we had best act

like its coming so if it does come it wont take us by
surprise and if it dont it dont matter.

I stood the first watch while Dundee slept or
appeared to. I had a funny feeling that his eyes wasnt
all the way shut and that he was peering out at me all
the time he was acting like he was off in the Land of
Nod. It made the hairs on the back of my neck stand
up. Dundee was like I seen him the first time looking
like he was a Cougar all set to pownse.

Once when I didnt even know it my eyes shut on me
and I dont know was it a minnit or an hour had gone
by with them shut when I heard Dundee say boy like a
growl and my eyes snapped open and they stayed wide
open for the rest of my watch.

When it come Dundees turn I just fell into bed and
was asleep fast. I dont know how long I had been
asleep when I felt a hard hand land on my shoulder
which woken me real fast. What is it I said blinking
from the light of the fire and sitting up. Is it soljers I
asked and Dundee said yes you take the back window
and I will take the front.

I went to the back window and looked out real
careful but I couldnt see a thing out there in the night.
My gun in my hand felt cold and heavy. Then there
was this voice like it come out of the Mouth of a Haunt
out there in the dark. Hallo the house it yelled. This is
Lutenant Nordell. We have you surrounded. Come out
and give up. It was soljers no doubt about that but I
still couldnt spot a One of them. You see anybody I
asked Dundee. Shut your Mouth he said lest you give
your position away.

Somebody outside fired a shot at the front of the
house. Dundee didnt shoot back. Then somebody fired
at the back. I cant see nobody I said forgetting to shut

my Mouth and Dundee said hold your fire until you can see what your shooting at.

Come out said the voice which was Lutenant Nordells. We have no wish to kill you but we will do so if you resist us.

I coffed and Dundee said god dam it. They have gone and blocked up the Chimny he said. I turned around and seen the smoke that was filling up the house from the fire we had going. We both took to coffing then and Dundee to cursing some more. He broke the window with the but of his gun and told me to do the same to the window where I was which I did. The fresh air that come in the windows helped some but not enuff to keep either me or Dundee from coffing. My eyes started watering so bad I could hardly see.

The smoke will kill us as dead as any bullets if we stay holed up in here Dundee said in between coffs. We have got to make a run for it. You go out that window and I will go out the door over here. Go out shooting he told me. Maybe we will make it. You reddy he asked me and when I said I was as reddy as I ever would be he yelled go and I went.

The cool night air outside was a Blessing and I drew some in to clear my Throat while I went running for the woods shooting every which way at nothing I could see. When my gun was empty I was still far from the woods but I didnt dare stop to reload it. I just kept on running and what I did was I run right into the arms of a soljer who was out there in the woods like he was waiting on me. I hit him with my gun barel but it didnt do him any harm. He just bent back my hand until I dropped the gun and then he marched around to the front of the house where Dundee was standing with his back up against the wall and his hands up in the air. The soljers that had put the kibosh on me shoved me up alongside Dundee and I did like he was doing. Put my hands up and kept my mouth shut.

Did they hurt you he asked me out the side of his mouth.

No I said what about you. I am fine he said first and then he said so far. I knew what he ment. Lutenant Nordell and all the other soljers was making sport of us and laughing like we was a joke somebody had told them.

Get there horses from the barn Lutenant Nordell ordered and Two of the soljers went to do his bidding. Pretty soon they come back with our horses all Saddled and Lutenant Nordell ordered us to climb on board which we both did and then Lutenant Nordell told us to move out which we also did with soljers riding on both the left and the right of us.

We headed west and I reckoned we was being taken over to the Kansas side of the border where the soljers and the Jayhawkers both come at us from. We rode for quite a while without nobody saying nothing. The moon was allmost down when Dundee started in to crowding me. He moved his horse close up to mine. I was just about to move over to give him room when he said low stay put. Then he said I am going to start something. When I do you look sharp and if you get so much as haff a chanse make a run for it.

He moved away from me then so I couldnt ask him any Questions lest the soljers should hear me. All I could do was keep on riding and wait for Dundee to make his move. He did some time later when he was in among some trees where it was even darker than out in the open. He all of a sudden reached out and grabbed the bit iron of the soljers horse that was on his right. He give it a jerk and the horses head swung around and it screamed something awful. Then it reared and threw the soljer that was riding it. Dundee hit the horse hard in the head with his Fist and it sprung forward knocking into the horse ahead of it. That horses rider lost control of his mount for a minnit and that minnit was enuff for Dundee to give him a shove and knock him clean out the Saddle.

There was shouting then with Lutenant Nordell yelling for somebody to stop Dundee. But there was no stopping him. Just before I made a break for it when the line of soljers on my left broke to go get Dundee I saw him and somehow or another he had got a rifle in his hands and he was swinging it this way and that and soljers was going down like Ten Pins.

I rode then like I never have rode before or sinse. Like the wind I went. I hung on to my reins for dear life and prayed that I wouldnt fly out the Saddle which I didnt meening that my prayers was ansered.

I looked back over my shoulder once and I seen Dundee leave those soljers behind him and head in my direction. But I didnt slow down any. I figured he could catch up with me being the good Horseman that he was so I just kept putting my heels to my horse and he kept going as game as could be.

Next time I looked back I didnt see Dundee. I figured maybe he had gone to ground to hide out from the soljers which would have been a smart thing to do. I desided then and there that that was what I had best do so I found myself an overhang under a ridge where some bushes was growing. I drew rein and then me and my horse went into the bushes and I hunkered down in my hidey hole. The only thing that worryed me was my horse. He was blowing hard and I didnt know no way to quiet him. I prayed for no soljers to come and hear him and again my prayers was ansered. No soljers come.

By dawn I had seen no sign of Dundee. I figured I had best be moving on but I didnt know where to go. I knew where I wanted to go but I werent so sure it would be the smart thing to do to go back to the homeplace on account of the soljers might come there hunting me. But where else could I or should I go I wondered and my wondering got me to the point where I said dam it I got to go there. Where else would I be likely to meet up with Dundee. Where else would he be likely to go to. Besides which my gun was back there where I had lost it when the soljer knocked it out my hand. So was Dundees brush gun back there and both of them Weppons we would need sinse I seen when they caught us that somebody had took Dundees sidearm off of him. I let my horse browse the bushes a bit in the early morning light and then I pointed him at the homeplace and there we went stopping only long enuff for me to water him at a crick we forded along the way.

The first thing I done when I got home was to go hunting my gun which took me no time at all to find. The next thing I did was to load it and then I got a ladder from the barn and climbed up on the roof where I found out that the soljers had put an army blanket over the chimny and tyed it in place to Smoke us out. I took off the rope and threw it and the blanket down to the ground. I climbed down and went inside the house where it smelled something awful of Smoke and where things had got black from the Smoke and made the place a pure mess. I got a bucket of water

from the stream and some cloths and started to clean
house. I didnt get very far by the time the sun was
down so I give it up telling myself tomorrow was
another day. I eat some crakkers and drunk some
Coffee and when I was done Dundee still hadnt
showed himself.

That didnt sit right with me at all. He should have
come by now I knew only I wondered what if he had
desided to go someplace else like to the Weavers where
they was in Winston up in Clay county. It being that
Dundee was so smitten with Miss Cordelia that might
be the case I thought to myself but then I desided no
that didnt make sense on account of he wouldnt have
wanted to leave the homeplace with nobody to protekt
it. Well maybe he somehow knew he had me to do that
chore. But how could he know that for sure I asked
myself and the anser I give myself was he couldnt
know. Not for sure he couldnt.

Thats when I got to feeling fidgety.

I thought back to what had happened. I went over it
all in my mind like I was seeing pictures in there. The
last picture was of Dundee riding away from the
soljers toward me which was the last time I seen him.

What if they shot him down in his tracks I thought
and got a sick feeling inside.

I tryed then to stop thinking and just wait but that
didnt work worth a dam. I made up my mind I had to
do something only I didnt know what. I only knew I
couldnt just sit and twiddle my thums. I had to find
Dundee. Or at least find out what had happened to
him. Nothing happened to him I told myself as I
climbed back into the Saddle. He may have gone to
town to buy things we was needing. That give me an
idea.

I went to town. When I got there it was closed up just about. Houses had no lights where people was either hiding in the dark or like in the case of One I seen where the front door was wide open to the night they had lit a shuck on account of the army Notise about the burning. I didnt know where to go or what to do until I remembered Louise. I went to her house but there was no anser to my knock on the door and no Lamps lit inside. I peered in through the window and couldnt see no tables or chairs. I knew then she was gone for sure and I wondered would I ever see her again.

On my way back into the middle of town I heard riders and I went for my gun wondering was they soljers. It turned out they was just ordinary men and when they saw me One of them drew rein and said what you doing out here in the middle of the night boy. Dont you know the army meens to burn this town down come tomorrow.

Yes sir I know that I said but I come here on the lookout for a friend of mine. His names Dundee.

A whisper like a little wind went among the men and then the man who had spoke to me said you must be Jubal Bonner.

Yes sir I am I said. How come you know me.

I heard from Augie Lambert that you were with Dundee the man said. I am afraid I have got some bad news for you Bonner.

Oh please dont let Dundee be dead I prayed and the man said the army had Dundee locked up across the border in Freemont.

Are you sure about that I asked. I meen Dundees not dead is he.

Us boys was over there in Kansas today the man

said. We set us a few fires of our own over there to
warm up those Jayhawkers some. Give them a taste of
the Hell they are heading for. Thats where we heard
the news that the army took Dundee and threw him in
jail in Freemont.

I am obliged to you for the news I told the man and
then went riding out of town heading for the border.

I didnt know what I was going to do when I got
there but I knew One thing for sure I wasnt doing
Dundee no good where I was.

I hadnt gone more than Two or Three miles when I
fell out of the Saddle on account of I had gone to sleep
in it. I hurt my shoulder but I didnt mind. I was
allmost glad of the hurt which helped me stay awake
for the rest of my ride.

I finally give up on any more night riding for Two
reasons. One was I was asleep haff the time in the
Saddle and didnt want to fall out of it again and maybe
bust my head the next time and the other reason was I
hadnt the foggiest notion of where Freemont was.

I drew rein and picketed my horse. Then I rolled up
snug as a Bug in my Saddle blanket and got me some
shut eye. When I woken it was near to noon I could
tell by where the sun was at in the sky. So I got on my
horse and rode west. The first farmhouse I seen in the
distance I went over to and asked the folk that come
out when I halloed it where was Freemont. They told
me and I headed for the town which was no great
shakes I seen once I got to it. The first thing I did was
ride down the main street looking for the jail which I
remembered was the place Miss Cordelia had said
Jesse Dean Withers had eskaped out of.

That rememberanse made hope rise up in my heart.
If Mister Withers could eskape out that jail I thought

then maybe so could Dundee with me to lend him a hand. I remembered Miss Cordelia said Mister Withers stole himself a horse after he had eskaped. That made me wonder what had happened to Dundees horse.

I looked around and seen the Livery down on the other side of the street so I went over to it after leaving my horse hitched to a rail across from the jail. I went in and looked around and there in a stall was Dundees horse. The man in the livery asked me what did I want and I told him I didnt want nothing and left.

If Dundee was to make good his getaway once he was out of the Freemont jail he would need a horse I thought to myself. A horse and a gun.

I walked back to my spot across the street from the jail and I stood there pondering my next move.

What I needed to know was if there was any soljers in that jail who might know me by sight. So over to the jail I went and bold as brass I peered in the window. There wasnt a single soljer to be seen inside the jail. Just a man with his Boots up on an old desk that had seen better days. He was wearing a Six gun and a star on his shirt so I pegged him for the Sherriff. Back behind him was a row of Two cells in One of which was Dundee lying down on a bunk on a mattress that had Corn shucks falling out it. The other cell was empty.

I went back across the street and stood there looking at the old jail like I was trying to memorize it. And all the while I was doing that my thoughts was racing around in my head like Hounds after a rabbit. The rabbit was what was I going to do to bust Dundee out of that jail. It wasnt until I had went into the Saloon down the block and had me a drink of Whisky that the

Hounds in my head caught that rabbit they was chasing.

I held up my empty Glass and the Bar Dog come over and filled it up. I hear the army caught up with that Missouri Marawder name of Dundee I said to the Bar Dog and he said thats a fact. I heard tell about Dundee more than once I said. Meen sonofabitch folk say he is. No wonder it taken the whole army to run him down. It will probably take an army to guard him to.

Not on your life says the Bar Dog to me. The army has better things to do. The Sherriff can keep an eye on his Prisoner.

Doesnt the Sherriff have any Deputys I said.

Doesnt need any said the Bar Dog. We dont have much Crime here in Freemont. This is a peesable town by and large.

When the Bar Dog went to see to another customers wants I put some money on the bar and leaving my second Whisky untouched behind me so I would be almost as sober as Sunday for what I had to do next I left the Saloon and went back to where I had been watching the jail from.

My head was swimming from the One whisky I had drunk but I could see straight and walk straight and all in all I was feeling on top of the world in fact I felt a little like laughing. So I desided now was as good a time as any to do what needed doing. I up and walked across the street and through the door of the jail.

The Sherriff looked up and said what can I do for you and I drew my gun and said you can hand over that gun of yours. His Boots come down off of the desk with a bang and he went for his gun. I put a bullet in the wall on One side of him which made him say dont shoot and put his hands up. Dundee got up from his bunk in his cell and give me a look I couldnt read.

Howdy I said to him and then to the Sherriff I said open up that cell.

The Sherriff got up and took a key ring down off of a nail and opened Dundees cell. I went up behind the Sherriff and told him to hand over his gun and kartridge belt to Dundee which he did.

Dundee strapped the belt on and then moving swift he ripped the Sherriffs Shirt and used peeses of it to tie the mans hands behind his back and then his Ankles. He stuffed a peese in the Sherriffs Mouth to gag him and threw him into the cell he had been in. He locked it and threw the keys across the room.

Your horse is in the Livery barn I said to him as I put my gun back in my holster. I reckon we had best go get it. I reckon your right he said. We left the jail and I got my horse and the pair of us strolled down the street.

When we was inside the Livery barn and the Livery man come up to us Dundee said to me you hold your gun on him while I get my horse reddy to ride.

I drew my gun and the Livery man made a sound in his Throat like he was going to scream so I told him dont and he didnt. It taken Dundee only a few minnits to get his horse all set and then the Two of us was out of the livery and riding down the street and out of town with the sun at our backs and nothing but Freedom in front of us.

After we had crossed the border Dundee drew rein. I followed him in among some trees where it turned out there was a crick. We got out our Saddles and was watering our horses when Dundee said how in the sam hill did you manage that.

If you meen how did I bust you out of the jail back there it was easy. You saw how I did it.

No he said I meen how did you know where I was.

I told him about going to town and meeting the men One of whom at leest knew me and how he told me he had heard where Dundee was.

I thought all along you was somewhere on my backtrail I told him. But when night come and you didnt show up back at the homeplace I said I got worryed and went into town to see if you had gone there. Thats when I met those men like I told you. I was glad to hear that you wasnt shot or wurse.

Maybe wurse would have been better Dundee said. I asked him what he ment on account of what he said sounded like pure crazyness to me.

I cant stand being cooped up in a jail he said. Never could.

I didnt say anything for a minnit then as we hunkered down while our horses grazed the Spring Clover that was in bloom all along the banks of the crick. But I did a lot of thinking. From the way Dundee had ansered me it seemed plain enuff that he had been in jail before he was in jail over in Freemont. I wanted to ask him where and when and why and like that but Dundee wasnt the kind of man you could put a whole lot of Questions to. Besides to ask all that would amount to prying and my Pa used to say a man had all he could do to mind his own Business without trying to mind other peoples.

I start to wither up and die Dundee said when I am all cooped up. I reckon it has something to do with how I allways have been a man who needs to see whats up around the bend in the crick and over the mountain. It comes from being a country boy I reckon.

I know what you meen I said on account of I am a country boy to.

When he didnt say nothing more I said do you know where we are going.

To the homeplace he said.

Are you sure thats such a good idea I asked him. If those soljers come after us once they sure enuff could come twise or even more times until they bag us again.

I know that Dundee said. But I have it in mind to round up some reinforsements.

Who and how many I asked him.

Anybody I can find who is willing he ansered.

The homeplace is a mess I said. Its all smokee and it smells bad but we can clean it up with some soap and water and a little Elbo greese. I allreddy started to only I give up to go on the prowl for you.

I want to tell you I am glad you did Dundee said. They had me dead to rights and there was talk of a necktie party down the road aways.

They ment to hang you I asked and he nodded and said there was talk of sedition and me being a traytor. Dam it I am no more a traytor than Major Parkinson himself is. There is something about vengefull men that makes them see things all crooked.

I asked him what had happened to land him in the Freemont jail. I told him the last time I seen him he was free and clear of all those soljers.

Thats true I was he said but then I had the bad luck to run into an army scout that come riding in at an angle and when he saw all those blubellys chasing me he cut me off and they caught up with me. They werent taking any chanses with me after our little fracas. They tyed my hands behind my back and my ankles under the belly of my horse.

Dundee didnt say any more and pretty soon we rode out and we hadnt gone far when we spotted some soljers off in the distance. He give me a signal and both of us headed for the nearest cover. We hid our horses and got behind some rocks and waited for the soljers to ride by us. Just about the time they come near to us my horse taken to nickering and then so did Dundees like the Two Beests was carrying on a regular conversation. Dundee skooted over to his horse and clapped his hands over its Nostrils moshuning me to do the same to mine which I did. Now that was a trick I never knew before about how to keep a horse quiet. It worked fine.

The soljers come and they went. The strange thing about them though was they had a woman riding with them. When we set out again I asked Dundee what did he think that woman was with the soljers for and he said for no good. I wasnt sure what he ment by that so I let the matter drop.

When we come to the Bantry place we seen it was burnt down to the ground and was just a heep of smoking ashes and a few charred timbers. The yard was full of chickens with there heads cut off and lying underfoot. A trunk lay open in the yard and dresses and a cutaway coat was stroon about all over the ground. So was some photographs of Mr. and Mrs. Bantry from days gone by. They had been stepped on and there Frames broken to bits.

Do you think was it soljers I said to Dundee and he said no doubt as he sat his Saddle with his big hands rapped around his Saddle horn.

Then they wasnt fooling with that Notise they put up I said.

I never for a moment thought they were Dundee

said. Then he rammed his Boots into his horses flanks and taken off like the wind. I had to hurry to catch him up which I didnt do until we was close to the homeplace. It was as we kept galloping along like we was late for Sunday meeting or something that it hit me why Dundee was in such a rush and I got a fearfull feeling that left a sour taste in my Mouth.

My wurst fear was turned into a fact when we got to the homeplace and found it in ashes and still Smoking. I couldnt take my eyes off of it. Dundees brush gun lay in the middle of the ashes with its barel sticking up. Here and there was peeses of Metal such as spoons gone all black from the fire and there was our Kettle laying where the Chimny still stuck up out of the roons. The barn to was burned down and so was our Corn.

But the wurst thing of all was the way somebody had went and kicked over the Cross that marked where Dundees mothers Grave was behind where the house had been.

CHAPTER 9

Dundee got down off of his horse and went to where his Ma was buryed. He set the Cross right side up again over her Grave. Then he went into the roons unmindfull of how they was still smoldering in places and when he come back he was carrying his brush gun and tossing it back and Fourth from hand to hand on account of I reckon it was still hot.

He stuck it into his Saddle Boot and then he looked at me and said I dont want you to think I am not gratefull to you for how you got me out of that jail over in Freemont but this is where we part company.

How come I asked him.

On account of I have things I have to do he ansered.

What things I asked him.

I am heading north he ansered.

North to where I asked him.

Winston up in Clay county he ansered.

To see Miss Cordelia I take it I said.

No he said to hook up with Augie Lambert and his boys.

What for I asked him.

I am going to ride with them he said.

What for I said.

I meen to show Major Parkinson and Lutenant Nordell and all there soljers that they dont burn me out and get away with it. I want revenge for this he said and pointed to the roons of the homeplace. For this and for them jailing me and talking about stretching my neck.

I have no love for the army either after what they done here I said so I wouldnt mind hooking up with Augie Lambert for the same reason you meen to.

No he said. I have let you hang around to long as it is. I dont want your Blood on my hands boy.

I am not a boy so stop calling me One I said getting hot under the collar. And another thing I said. What makes you think my Blood will be on your hands if any of it should happen to get spilled. He started in to say something but I cut him off. I can take care of myself I said. What I do isnt somebody elses fault.

It seems we dont see things the same way he said. But lets set that matter to One side. The thing is I am riding alone from here on in. I dont want you around any more.

You claimed you wasnt ungratefull to me for what I done for you over to Freemont I said mad as a wet hen. Well I will tell you something Dundee. As far as I am conserned you are just about the most ungratefullest so and so I ever did meet. I went and put my neck on the block for you over to Freemont and what did it get me. It got me the Boot thats what it got me. Your Boot I meen. It got me my walking papers. If thats not ungratefull then you show me what the Hell is.

Dundee just looked at me with those peersing eyes of his and I tryed my best not to blink in the face of them but I did anyway. Then he turned his horse and rode north.

I watched him until he was out of sight and all that time he never once looked back.

I took One last look at the burned Corn I would

never now get to taste. Then I turned my horse and rode west which is the way I had been heading when I first run into Dundee. Like him I didnt look back so much as once though I wanted to real bad.

The sun was down when I come upon a farmhouse this side of the border. I rode up to it and called out but nobody come out. So I went to the door and knocked. Nobody ansered. I looked around and it didnt take me long to find out the place was deserted. I looked all through the kitchen but there was no food to be found except some dryed out bread that had weevils eating at it. I brushed them away along with the Webs that they had spun in the bread and then I eat it all. It was either that or go hungry.

I went and took my horse out to the barn where I stalled him and stripped him of my gear and put some Oats I found in a feed bin for him. Then I went back inside the house. I took off my gun and slept the sleep of the dead in a stripped down rope bed.

I dreemed about Dundee. But what I dreemed I clean forgot when I woken and found the house on fire all around me.

I jumped up and grabbed my gun and made for the door but that was no good I soon seen on account of the flames was coming up the stairs to the second floor. I run the other way down the hall and could feel the heet of the fire on my back and I could hear the floor under my feet starting to crak which ment that the downstairs was burning up fast. There was a window at the end of the hall. I busted it and looked out. There was a little overhang and I climbed out onto it and then sort of slid down it to the ground twisting my ankle when I hit but not so bad I couldnt stand up.

I was just getting on my feet when around the side

of the house come a soljer. When he seen me he froze.
So did I at first. But then I went for my gun. So did he
go for his. He got his out before I got mine out and he
said drop it which I had to do seeing as how he had me
dead to rights.

Lissen I said when I seen other soljers heading for
the barn. My horse is in there. The soljer only said
march and I marched around the house. As I did One
of the soljers that was reddy to burn the barn yelled
Major Parkinson. Thats when I seen Major Parkinson
for the first time and I thought I am a goner now for
sure when he sees me.

Theres a horse in here sir the soljer told Major
Parkinson. Maybe there is somebody belonging to it
inside the house.

I allmost laughed at that. Here the house was
burning like a Torch and they taken to wondering was
anybody inside of it.

Didnt you check to make sure Corporel that the
house was empty before you set it on fire Major
Parkinson asked.

The soljer who had his gun on me butted in and said
I found this Fellow jumping out of the house sir.

Major Parkinson turned and looked at me and
started to smile sort of. Well if it isnt now dont tell me
I shall remember your name in a moment oh yes its
Jubal Bonner isnt it.

I didnt say it was or it wasnt.

Major Parkinson called out Lutenant Nordell and
there come the Lutenant from out the Smoke like One
of Lucifers fallen Angels. Well well he said what have
we here meening me.

A stroke of Luck said Major Parkinson to Lutenant
Nordell. Dundee may have flown the Coop but now

we have his partner who will I am sure be able to tell us where to find him.

My horse is in the barn I said to nobody in particular. You fixing to burn him to death like you allmost did me.

An oversight Bonner Major Parkinson said. My men it would seem did a less than careful check of the house before they Torched it. Then he give an order and One of the soljers brought my horse and gear out the barn. He had the bridle on and it was a good thing he was a strong One else that horse would have dragged him from here to Kingdom Come on account of when it seen the fire that was making the sky red and sending peese of burning ash falling down on us all he tryed to break loose but the soljer held tight to him and he couldnt.

Was there anyone in the house with you Lutenant Nordell asked me.

If there was I ansered they are burned to a crisp by now. I thought I might as well let him know I had no intent of giving him or the Major any straight ansers about anything especially about Dundee.

Burn the barn Major Parkinson ordered his men and burn it they did.

The smell of Smoke was enuff to choke a person and the air all around was hot and the sky was part red from the fire and part black from the Smoke and hardly blu at all nor could you see the sun anywhere in it which made me wonder how long I had slept and what time was it. All I knew for sure was it was day.

Its time we were moving on Major Parkinson said and with that Lutenant Nordell give some orders and pretty soon we was riding out leaving the roons of the house and barn to Smoke and settle into Sinders behind us.

I wondered where they was taking me but I didnt ask. Even if I did I dont reckon they would have told me. I thought about the jail over to Freemont but that wasnt where we was headed I found out when we got far enuff from the fires so I could see the sun. We was heading east into it.

We come to a log Cabin and thats when the shooting started. Somebody inside it started shooting at the soljers and Lutenant Nordell give an order and the soljers started shooting right back. When that didnt get anybody any where Lutenant Nordell give another order and One of the soljers sneeked into the woods. Next time I seen him he come creeping out the woods. He climbed up on the Cabin roof and tyed a army blanket over the Chimny same as had been done at the homeplace to Dundee and me. In just a few minnits a man and woman and Two small girls come coffing out the Cabin with there hands in the air and with there eyes watering real bad.

Oh dont do it cryed the woman when she seen Two soljers One inside and One out put matches to the Cabin. Oh please dont do it she cryed fit to break the Heart of a Stone. But they went and did it anyway.

When the Cabin was burning bright Lutenant Nordell give an order and everybody moved out me among them with One soljer aiming his gun at the back of my head. Behind us we left the log Cabin folk weeping and wailing mostly the Two girls and the woman but the man he had Tears in his eyes to I seen. The soljers burned Three more places that day before Major Parkinson called it quits and give an order to head back to camp.

We crossed the border at sundown and come quick to where they had there camp. The first thing I seen surprised me. I didnt know what in the world to make of it. In the camp was Two women One of which was Missus Bantry who was Mister Asa Bantrys wife and the other was the One I seen riding with the soljers when I was still with Dundee. Why I wondered had the army taken them women Prisoners like they did me. Taking me Prisoner I could understand but why women was way beyond me.

When Missus Bantry seen me she started to come over to me but there was a soljer with a gun who I reckon was guarding her and the other woman with her and he stopped her in her tracks. I said to the soljer who had his gun on me I know that lady. Would it harm anybody if I went over and said hello to her. The soljer swore but he let me go over to Missus Bantry and she said oh Jubal I am so glad to see you but at the same time I am sorry to see you here.

How be you Missus Bantry I said and then wished I hadnt on account of I could see how she was which wasnt to good. Her hair was all askew and there was dirt on her hands and face and her dress was torn. She didnt anser my Question. Insted she asked me was I allright. I said I was and then she said how is Dundee and I said I cant anser you that. When she wanted to know why not I told her on account of Dundee and me had parted company.

They burned our place she told me and I said yes I seen that they did and she started in to cry with both dirty hands over her face. I didnt know what in the world to do or say to try to Comfort her. So I just stood there and waited for her to stop crying which after awhile she did and said she was sorry.

I said there aint no need to be sorry for weeping over such an awful loss. I know how hard it hurts. They burned our homeplace to I said. I meen they burned Dundees homeplace.

Oh no she said.

What happened to Mister Bantry I asked her or is he around here somewhere.

No he isnt she said. I dont know where he is. When the army came they took us by surprise. Asa tryed hard to fight them but there were so many of them there was little he could do. They made sport of him. One would knock him down and then when he got up again another would do the same thing. Finally they beat him senseless and left him there after setting fire to our home.

She started in to crying again before she could finish telling me her tale of woe. Then she caught her breath and said I have the most god awful thoughts. Sometimes I am afraid that the beating they gave poor Asa might have killed him. Or that he is dazed and wandering about somewhere with no idea of who he is or what has happened.

I didnt know what to say to that so I asked who is that other woman over there. Missus Bantry said that is Missus Cronun. She is a widow and she lived all alone Four miles East of Asa and me.

One of the soljers come out a tent then and he had a Bottle in his hand. I seen he was drunk. He looked at Missus Bantry and she stepped closer to me and then he looked at Missus Cronun and then he took a swig from his Bottle.

He was in plain sight of both Major Parkinson and Lutenant Nordell but neither One of them payed him no mind drunk as he was. He staggered over to Missus

Cronun who said leave me be but he wouldnt. He pulled her to him and put his Bottle to her Mouth but she pushed it away. He tryed again to make her take a swig from his Bottle but she wouldnt so he give up trying and dragged her into his tent. You couldnt help hearing the words he said to her on account of how loud he was talking. They was bad words maybe the wurst I ever heard and I couldnt beleeve he was saying them to a woman.

I tryed talking to Missus Bantry but it was hard on account of the soljer in his tent was yelling and Missus Cronun was screaming. When after awhile there wasnt any noise coming from either One of them Missus Bantry and I tryed talking hopefull about the Future as best we could. She mostly asked me about mine. I told her I was heading west. California maybe I said. I have never seen the oshun they got out there though I seen pictures of it I told her.

They say it is lovely there Missus Bantry said. They say it is warm there.

Thats the way it went with us for awhile with neither of us saying much of anything and sertenly not what was most on our minds. In her case I reckon that was what had happened to her husband and what was happening to the woman in the tent with the drunken soljer. With me it was what was they fixing to do with me and wishing Dundee hadnt of turned me loose like he did though I didnt blame him sinse I knew he had done it to try to keep me out of harms way while at the selfsame time he went and put himself in it.

Night come and the soljers made a big fire. The lot of them sat around it drinking and eating but mostly drinking. One of them brought me and Missus Bantry some food. It was beans and Rice. Missus Bantry didnt eat any of hers but I Wulfed mine down and could have done with some more but I wouldnt ask those soljers for seconds.

Right about then the soljer who had took Missus Cronun come out his tent buttoning up his pants. He still had his Bottle and he drunk from it on his way over to the fire. Pretty soon Missus Cronun come out the tent and I seen how her dress was ripped. I looked down at Missus Bantrys dress where it was ripped to. She seen me looking at it and left me to go over to Missus Cronun and help her to sit down on the ground.

As the night wore on things got boysturus. The soljers was still drinking out of Bottles and Jugs they had and sometimes One of them or maybe Two at a time would come over to where we was and take One of the women away. When it was Missus Bantry they took I made like I was asleep where I was lieing on the ground so she wouldnt know I seen them take her.

Once when a soljer come for Missus Cronun I sat up and said why cant you leave her alone she has suffered enuff on account of you. The soljer that taken her just laughed at me and said you shut your Mouth boy. Theres at leest One man here who would just as soon take you insted of One of the women so dont go calling attenshun to yourself if you know whats good for you.

Thats the way things went for most of the night. But awhile before dawn come the soljers at last got less boysturus and finally they all went to sleep some of them passing out from the Red Eye they had drunk.

I slept some in fits and starts on account of all the noise from the soljers and the now and then wailing of the women and my own thoughts which was running wild in every direction so that I couldnt find no peese of mind. Mostly I was trying hard to make myself beleeve that things would all work out for the best in the end. When a Rifle in the ribs woken me I seen it was day but with the sun not yet in sight.

Major Parkinson wants to see you the soljer who had jabbed me with his Rifle said. On your feet he said.

I got up and he marched me to a big tent at the end of the line. He pushed me into it and there was Major Parkinson and Lutenant Nordell looking as fresh as dayzys. They was sitting down behind a long table but there werent no place for me to sit down so I stood there trying not to look scared of what they might have in mind to do to me. I still had not forgot how Miss Cordelia had told about them burning Mister Withers feet in a fire.

So this is the Whippersnapper who got Dundee out of jail said Major Parkinson. He looked at me like I was some ugly kind of Bug he had never seen before.

How did he know it was me I was wondering when he ansered my Question like as if he had read my mind.

The Sherriff of Freemont described you to us he said.

So we knew at once who had enjineered the escape Lutenant Nordell said.

I take it Dundee is a good frend of yours Major Parkinson said.

I didnt say a thing.

Lutenant Nordell stepped out real smart from behind the desk and he give me a slap that nearly knocked my head off of my shoulders. Anser the Major when he speaks to you skum he said.

My head was spinning as I said Dundee and me we was together for a spell thats all.

Are you saying you arent frends Major Parkinson asked and I said I reckon we was but we parted company.

There is a saying Major Parkinson said that I remember which has to do with frendship. Greater love hath no man than this that a man lay down his life for his frend he said.

I know that saying I said. Its from out the bible.

Would you lay down your life for your friend Dundee Lutenant Nordell asked me in a sly voice.

I didnt know how to anser that and I didnt have to on account of just then Major Parkinson said we want to know where we can find Dundee.

What for I asked do you still meen to hang him.

We must make an example of him Major Parkinson said without ansering my Question I notised. He must not be allowed to escape army Justise.

Mister Jesse Dean Withers escaped it I said trying to get the Majors mind off of Dundee.

Lutenant Nordell took to grinning before he said Mister Jesse Dean Withers is dead. We met again Two days ago while he was with some other men raiding here in Kansas. I was the One who shot him to death.

So you see said Major Parkinson I spoke the Truth before when I spoke of army Justise. Now tell me Bonner where Dundee is.

I dont know where he is I said which was allmost True though I knew he was headed for the town of Winston in Clay county but I didnt know had he got there yet.

Major Parkinson spoke to Lutenant Nordell then saying do you beleeve him.

I do not Lutenant Nordell said. Then he boxed my ears for me until I saw stars.

Bonner be a good Fellow and tell us what we want to know Major Parkinson said. There was something about his eyes that made me think he was liking what he saw when Lutenant Nordell boxed my ears. You will save us time and yourself any more unplesentness. I didnt like One bit the sound of that last part but I said to myself what would Dundee do was he standing here in my shoes and the anser was as plain as the nose on my face. He wouldnt tell them a dam thing. So I kept my Mouth shut.

Major Parkinson got up and come around to stand in front of me. He shook a finger in my face and said we can make things very unplesent for you you know. Why forse us to do that. Is Dundee so important to you that you would suffer what we can make you suffer if you do not tell us what we want to know. What is he but just another Southern Sympathizer of no more worth than the Missouri mule his Stuborness makes him rezemble.

I got so mad at what the Major had said I spit in his face before I even knew what it was I was doing.

Dam you Lutenant Nordell shouted at me. He grabbed my right arm and twisted it up behind my back. I gritted my teeth as he twisted it some more. How dare you do such a thing to your betters he said. I will show you how skum like you should behave in front of a man like Major James Parkinson who is One of the best offisers in the entire United States Army.

With his other hand Lutenant Nordell grabbed me by the back of the neck. He forsed me down on my knees in front of Major Parkinson. I fought hard to get back up but I couldnt budge on account of the Lutenants grip on me was so strong.

Your not even fit to lick the Majors Boots Lutenant Nordell yelled at me.

The Major laughed and said but maybe we should let him lick them anyway. What do you think Lutenant.

At that Lutenant Nordell started smiling the same evil way as Major Parkinson was doing. The next minnit he forsed my head down low toward the Majors Boots. Major Parkinson moved One of his Boots up close to my face. I tryed to turn my head to One side but I couldnt on account of how Lutenant Nordell was holding so tight to my arm and neck.

Do it the Lutenant ordered me. I stuck out my tongue to make like I was going to lick the Majors Boot that he had near my Mouth thinking maybe that would make Lutenant Nordell let go of me only it didnt. I had ment to make a run for it but sinse he still had a hold of me what I did was punch the Major between the legs with my One free hand.

Major Parkinson jumped back and let out a howl like a Wulf does on a full moon night.

Lutenant Nordell kicked me in the but. Then he hit me up alongside the head and he said I will fix this skum Major. He dragged me out of the tent and he called some soljers over and he give them there orders and by the time those soljers was through with me my Shirt was off and my arms was rapped around a tree and tyed tight there. My chest was up against the trunk of the tree and Lutenant Nordell had got a Cat Of Nine Tails in his hand and he was telling everybody to stand back and give him room.

Everything got real quiet then while I waited for what I knew was coming. But it didnt come. Not at first it didnt. What did come was the sound of Major

Parkinsons voice. He was out of my sight behind me when he said Bonner I will overlook that little insident in my tent just now and see to it that you are not flogged if you will tell me where to find Dundee.

I dont know where he is if he is alive I said but if he isnt alive you might try looking for him down in the halls of Hell.

I heard a soljer snikker and at the same time I heard Major Parkinson say to Lutenant Nordell proseed.

The first time the Cat hit me wasnt so bad though it did smart a lot. The second time wasnt all that bad neither. I meen I could still bear up under it. But the third time that leather tore into me it was awful how much Pain it brought. It slammed me up against the bark of the tree I was tyed to and after a few more strokes of that Cat my chest was Bleeding same as my back only not so bad.

I lost count of how many times I got lashed. I only know it was a lot. Things would start to go dark around me and then they would light up again. Through it all I could hear Major Parkinson counting the lashes as Lutenant Nordell layed the leather on me.

Enuff Major Parkinson said and Lutenant Nordell stopped flogging me. The Major come around to where I could see him out the corner of my eye and he said to me where is Dundee. I just shut my eyes and leened my cheek against the ruff bark of the tree trying to catch my breath and keep the sweat that was running down my face from getting inside my eyes.

When I opened my eyes again Major Parkinson was gone.

The Cat come down on my back again and it made

me bite my tongue which started to bleed in my Mouth.

I swore to myself that I wouldnt scream again. The Cat kept landing on my bare back and the Pain it left behind was like a fire burning every place in me. Even in my mind.

Stop it you will kill him I heard Missus Bantry cry out.

But Lutenant Nordell didnt stop it. He kept at it.

Still I didnt scream but to my ever lasting shame I heard myself say One word not much louder than a whisper. The word was Winston.

Hold on Major Parkinson said. Then he was alongside me again. He asked me did I say something and I said Winston again.

He bent down close to me and I said Dundee told me he was heading north to the town of Winston.

My voice give out on me at that point and I couldnt say no more.

Speak up Bonner Major Parkinson said. When I couldnt he grabbed a handfull of my hair and he shook my head till my teeth took to rattling in my Mouth.

If you will step aside sir said Lutenant Nordell from behind me I will give him another taste of the Cat.

Winston is in Clay county in Missouri I said real quick to the Major to keep that Cat at bay. He let loose of my hair and my face fell against the tree trunk.

What is Dundee doing there the Major asked me and I told him he ment to visit a family by the name of Weaver who had gone there to get out of the way of the burning.

Major Parkinson went away and I could hear him talking to somebody behind me which was probably

Lutenant Nordell and then everybody went away and left me there.

At leest I thought everybody had left only it turned out Lutenant Nordell hadnt. He come up alongside me and he said to me maybe now you have learned how to treat your betters skum. If you ever do such a thing again to a man as noble and just as Major Parkinson I will kill you with my bear hands not just flog you. Major Parkinson is a fine man and a fine soljer he said. I worship the very ground he walks on. It is an honor to serve under him and to carry out his orders.

He said some more things about how he felt about the Major. He had a wild look in his eyes all the time he talked like a man mad in love with a woman or a Hellfire and Brimstone Preacher in love with his god. Or like a crazy man in One of his Fits.

After awhile I couldnt hear what he was saying nor did I care to. My eyes was on the leather Cat he still had in his right hand which wasnt black no more but red with my Blood.

Then it was gone and so was Lutenant Nordell. I hung limp there on the tree wondering what was coming next. I couldnt think straight though on account of the Pain that was like somebody had made me lay down on my back on a bed of hot coals.

Then little by little the dark started coming back. I sunk down into it to a place where I couldnt feel any Pain which was a Blessing.

CHAPTER 10

When I come to myself a long time later judging by
where the sun was in the sky I felt Pain again and it
werent all in my back where Lutenant Nordell had
flogged me with his Cat Of Nine Tails. It was also in
my mind and laying heavy on my heart. I meen the
Pain I felt on account of how I had went and spilled
the beans about where Dundee was at or at leest
supposed to be at from what he had told me when we
parted company. It was hard for me to tell which kind
of Pain was hurting me the most.

I looked around me from where I was laying on the
ground by the tree I had been tyed to. Somebody had
cut me loose while I was out of this world and left me
lying there. I could see the tents and the ashes where
the fire had been the night before. I couldnt see sign of
either Missus Bantry or Missus Cronun. I didnt know
was they in the tents or out riding with the soljers. I
knew most of the soljers was gone on account of I
could count but Two or Three meandering around in
the camp. Also most of the horses was gone from the
rope corral.

But mine wasnt gone I seen for which I was
gratefull. Now I just had to get my hands on him and
get out of the camp and head for Clay county to find
Dundee and warn him about the trouble on his
backtrail.

The minnit I made a move my body betrayed me same as I had betrayed Dundee. Pain flashed through me and its torment was truly something feerse. But I couldnt let it stop me or for that matter even slow me down. So I got up on my knees and then got around behind the tree where I found my Shirt that they had took off of me before the flogging started. I put it on and then I started through the woods working my way toward the rope corral. When I got to the edge of the woods I waited a little while until no soljers was looking my way and then I run across an open space and ducked down under the rope and there I was in among the horses they had left behind. I went to mine which the soljers had left Saddled. I untyed the rope from a tree and got aboard him and we went galloping out of the camp. Behind me I heard One of the soljers shout something but nobody started shooting at me. I reckon they figured I wasnt worth the bother. I reckon Major Parkinson had no more interest in me now that I had told him what he wanted to know. He had far bigger fish to fry. Namely Dundee.

As I rode I could feel the wounds left by Lutenant Nordells whip breaking open where they had crusted. Pretty soon my back was Bloody in places but I payed it no mind and just kept heading Northeast. My gut was grumbling like thunder so I kept my eyes peeled for something eatable. In a field I run across some sheep Sorrel which had not yet got its full growth it being but Six or so inches high. I dismounted and pulled some up and chewed on the leaves as I rode along. The tart taste was not exactly to my liking but the Sorrel was sure enuff better than nothing at all in my belly.

Before night come I found some Curly Dock and I

eat the leaves of the plants I pulled up for supper though they was more filling than tastee. That night I got so sick to my stomach I like to have dyed but I didnt. I reckon I had eat to many of those sheep Sorrel plants which my Ma used to grow in her kitchen Garden. She used to make a drink by boiling up the leaves of sheep Sorrel. You could drink the water when it cooled which was a little like Lemonaid. I should have known better than to eat so much of the Sorrel on account of we once had a Goat that got poisoned from eating to much sheep Sorrel. But what was I to do when there wasnt nothing else around to eat.

I rode all night and come morning I knew by asking a man I run into that I was in Clay county and the town of Winston was Six miles due North of where I was at. When I got to it my Heart sunk for what did I see on the North end of town but soljers passing in and out of a Saloon that was there. I recognized them as the Majors men. I quick rode down a alley and out of town by another way so as not to be spotted.

It took me hours to find the farm the Weavers was renting. When I knocked on the farmhouse door who should open it to me but Miss Cordelia herself. I allmost forgot my manners and grabbed her and hugged her I was that glad to see a frendly face but I didnt.

Before I could bid her the time of day she said oh Jubal I can hardly beleeve my eyes is it reely you and I said yes it reely is and she said come in. I asked her was Dundee here and when she said he was I was releeved to hear the news and to know I wouldnt have to go traipsing all over Hells haff acre hunting him.

But he has been wounded she said.

What happened I asked her and she said I will let him tell you about it.

Oh she said then as she shut the door. Whatever happened to your back. I told her and she said oh my thats just awful let me put some heeling Salve on it.

Not now I said sounding blunt but not meening to. Could I talk to Dundee first I asked her and she said yes if you like. He is in the back of the house. She led the way and I followed her and on the way I seen somebody pass by the window outside. I guess I give a start on account of Miss Cordelia said thats Marcus. He is keeping an eye on things out there.

Then we come to a little bitty buttery in back that didnt seem big enough to hold a man like Dundee but there he was as big as life.

He give me One of those peersing looks of his and said to me what the Hell brought you here boy after I told you to skoot which just went to prove he was as full of sass as ever.

Dont think I come calling on you for the pure pleasure of it says I to him. I come to tell you it is time for you to git.

Dont be snappish with Jubal Miss Cordelia told Dundee. They have hurt him on your account.

What might that meen Dundee asked as suspishus as ever and I told him winding up with how I had told the soljers where he might be found hard as that was for me to do.

I will leave you Two alone Miss Cordelia said and left the buttery.

Let me see Dundee said so I turned around and taken off my Shirt. He took a long look at the raw meat Lutenant Nordell had made out of my back. He cussed under his breath at the sight and said that there needs seeing to.

Miss Cordelia said she had heeling Salve I told him.

He walked out of the room and just left me standing there. I was about to go after him a minnit or Two later when back he come with a china jar in One hand and a basin of water with a cloth soaking in it in the other. There was a bunk up against One wall and he told me to take off my Shirt and lay face down on it which I did.

Then he taken to washing the Blood off of my back and it hurt so bad I let out a yelp.

I got Salt in the water he said. Its good for what you have got. Even though the Salt water stung like Bees Dundee was gentle as a kitten with the washing of my wounds. For somebody with hands as big as Hams if I hadnt known who was looking after me I might have thought it was the gentlest of women folk. When he was done he spred Salve all over my back and then he got up and said sit up and let that stuff dry before you put your Shirt back on.

I sit up and tryed to look him in the eye but I couldnt. I said my peese anyhow. I told him I was sorry I had throwed in the Towl and told Major Parkinson where he might be at.

Never you mind about that he said. Pain has a way of making a man do things he wouldnt do were he not hurting. Pain is a wretched thing he said. It humbles us all One way or another before we get out of this old world. He give me a sidelong look and said you have nothing to be ashamed of. From the looks of the minsemeat they made out of your back it took a lot of strokes before they finally broke you. What counts is how long you stood them off not that you gave in at the end. I have known grown men in the army who went under the lash and didnt last past Two strokes before they broke. I am mighty proud of you for what you endured for me. I want you to know that.

It was what he said and it was how he said it that made all the hurting I had in me from Lutenant Nordells Cat Of Nine Tails seem worth while to me right then. To hear Dundee say what he did about me made me allmost willing to go through the whole thing again just to hear him say once more how he was proud of me.

Miss Cordelia told me you was wounded I said then. Do you mind telling me what happened.

I went to town yesterday to see what news there might be about the burning back home he said. I had the bad Luck to run into Major Parkinson in the Mercantile. He let out a holler when he saw me and then him and his soljers started chasing me. I gave them the slip and came back here by a roundabout way but not before One of them nicked me alongside my ribs. Which reminds me how is your leg these days.

Good as new I told him. What if the soljers find out where you are and come here looking for you I asked him.

Thats been on my mind sinse yesterday he ansered. When I got back here yesterday I told the Weavers I planned to ride out. Cordelia and Marcus and there Daddy wouldnt hear of me doing that. They prevaled on me to stay on account of I had Bled like a stuck Pig from my wound. So stay I did though against my better judgment. Old Mister Weaver has gone into town to find out what is going on with the army there. If he comes back with bad news I plan to move out of here fast.

I didnt know you knew the soljers was up here after you I said. I guess I wasted my time coming here to tell you what you allreddy knew.

You didnt waste your time Dundee said.

Didnt I I asked him.

No he said you didnt on account of to tell you the Truth I had got to the point where I had started feeling lonely and was cussing myself for running you off.

I looked close to see if he was smiling and making sport of me but he looked as sober as a Judge which give me the nerve to say I been lonesome to sinse we split up. But I reckon now its time for me to be moving on sinse I have done what I come up here to do.

I would be obliged to you if you would stay Dundee said.

Why I asked him.

Maybe we can keep each other out of any more trouble he said though somehow I doubt that. Any way we could sort of stick together and see how we like it he said.

I liked it fine before I said. If you hadnt of been so kantankerus I never would have left.

I guess I can be kantankerus at times he said.

And bullheaded to I said.

I pleed guilty he said.

But I am not allways so easy to get along with either I said so maybe you had cause to be kantankerus at times though I dont take the blame for you being bullheaded.

Are you hungry he asked me and I said I was.

He took me to the kitchen where Miss Cordelia was and she fryed up some Squirrel meat and boiled some

greens for me. Lutenant Nordell told me he shot Mr.
Withers to death I said and neither Miss Cordelia or
Dundee said nothing to that they only both looked
Grim. Is Augie Lambert up this way I asked and it was
Dundee told me no Augie was down south.

I had just finished the last of my eats when Marcus
Weaver come inside. He shook my hand and said how
Miss Cordelia had told him I was here.

Any sign of trouble out there Dundee asked him and
he said none.

It was the middle of the afternoon when Mister
Weaver come home with the bad news. He hardly
payed me no mind he was that upset over what he had
heard in town which was that the army had rounded
up all the men in town and was holding them under
guard.

What ever for Miss Cordelia asked him and he give
Dundee a look before ansering that Major Parkinson
had told everybody in town that he beleeved that some
of them knew where Dundee was hiding out at. They
are going to shoot every tenth man he said until
someone reveels your whereabouts he said.

Miss Cordelia went white as a Sheet and it looked to
me like she was reddy to pass out. They have no right
to do a thing like that she said. Someone must stop
them she said. They cannot shoot innosent people.

They can and they will unless I miss my guess
Mister Weaver said and she went even whiter.

Mister Weaver said to Dundee I should not have
been so open about your presense here. I should not
have introduced you to folk so openly as I did he said.
But I never for a moment thought that the army
would come here in pursoot of you.

Somebody is sure to spill the beans once the

shooting starts Marcus Weaver said and his sister said Dundee you must flee before that happens.

He didnt even appear to ponder what was said to him. He just up and announsed that he was going into town.

No you mustnt Miss Cordelia said.

They will shoot you on sight Marcus Weaver said.

When Dundee headed for the door I said wait. I am going with you.

I am to Marcus Weaver said.

So am I Mister Weaver said.

Dundee was at the door. He turned around and said I think it would be better if I went alone but you could see he was pleased that the Three of us was set on siding him.

Miss Cordelia run to Dundee and threw her arms around him. Dont go she said. Please dont go.

I will get our guns Marcus Weaver said and left the room. When he come back he give a gun to his Father and strapped One on himself.

I dont have a gun any more I told him. The soljers taken mine off of me. Do you think you could loan me One.

Marcus Weaver went and got me a gun which I was gratefull to get sinse I was pretty sure we was all Four of us heading straight for a Shooting Match.

We started for town leaving Miss Cordelia behind and I seen how she was full of fear for Dundee and for her kin and maybe for me to.

What are you going to do when we get to town Marcus Weaver asked Dundee as we rode along but Dundee didnt give him an anser.

We may be on a fools errand Mister Weaver said

sinse there seems to me to be no way to stop the army from doing this mad thing they have planned.

Mister Weaver and his Son come up with some ideas about what we should do but Dundee didnt say yes or no or maybe to any One of them. Me I tryed to come up with an idea of my own but had no Luck so I just kept my Mouth shut and hoped for the best which I reckoned might turn out to be that none of us would get ourselves killed when what I could see coming down the Pike at last got to us.

In town it was as quiet as a church on a Saturday night. There wasnt a Soul to be seen on the streets at first. But then out the Saloon and into what was left of the daylight come a bunch of soljers singing and clapping One another on the back like they was all good old boys together. They stopped short when they seen us. One of them pointed a finger at Dundee and said thats the basterd.

I want to see Major Parkinson Dundee said. Where is he he said.

Go get him One of the soljers said and another soljer lit out like a rabbit and run down the street.

Us Four we sat our Saddles and the soljers just stood there staring up at us. None of us had yet gone for our guns which I thought might be maybe a good sign.

Folk started coming out there houses and out the stores as if they had been waiting for something like this to happen. In no time at all there was the makings of a Crowd. I didnt know a Soul among them until who of all people should come riding into town but Mister Asa Bantry. I wanted to go over to him and tell him I seen his wife until I thought about the Questions he would ask me about Missus Bantry which I knew I didnt want to ever have to anser. Then I thought maybe she is with him now. Maybe the soljers turned her loose.

Dundee slid out of his Saddle at the same time as did Mister Bantry. The Weavers and me also stepped down to the ground. Then like Dundee we took up positions on One side of the street across from the soljers with the Crowd inkluding Mister Bantry off to one side where I couldnt see him. We just stood there and waited and pretty soon along comes Major Parkinson and Lutenant Nordell walking down the street like they owned it.

They stopped across the street from us where the Saloon and the soljers was. Major Parkinson said to Dundee have you come to surrender.

Yes I have Dundee said if that will stop you from shooting some of the men of this town.

I thought my Heart would stop.

People taken to whispering among themselves and I seen the glad looks on there faces which made me mad. If they had known Dundee like I did they wouldnt be so glad to see him turn himself in to the army and may be to a rope at the end of the line. But they didnt know him or care a Fig about him. All they cared about was there own selfs and there husbands and Sons and brothers and so on.

I thought our little plan might flush you out Major Parkinson said with a big smile on his face and I knew by that that Lutenant Nordell was in on the plan with him. I am glad you are being sensable he said to Dundee. Then he spoke over his shoulder to his soljers. I couldnt hear what he said but I reckoned here it comes and come it did.

The soljers drew there guns and started coming at us. Dundee started out to meet them.

Marcus Weaver grabbed him by the arm and said
dont do it but Dundee just shook him off. When he did
Marcus Weavers gun went off akksadental. Then
everything started happening real fast. One of the
soljers shot at us but didnt hit nobody. Dundee drew
his gun and took aim at Major Parkinson and said stop
the shooting. I went for my gun and fired it and so did
Dundee fire his when the shooting kept up on both
sides. Major Parkinson went down with Blood all over
his head on account of how Dundee had shot a peese
out of it.

Lutenant Nordell got down on One nee by the
Major and then he got back up and yelled dam you
Dundee. I am going to kill you for that.

I knew I had to act fast then so I run out and got in
front of Dundee and yelled at Lutenant Nordell you
got the wrong man you blind as a bat basterd. It was
me killed that no good Major of yours.

Lutenant Nordells eyes got big as Plates and spit
run out his Mouth in a foam. He taken aim at me and
Dundee said to him you shoot Bonner and I will shoot
you as dead as your Major Parkinson which made
Lutenant Nordell hold off and put down his gun.
Then Dundee said lets ride boy but before I could
make a move Lutenant Nordell give an order to take
me at the top of his voice and before you could say Jack
Frost In The Morning the soljers was all over me.
They taken my gun away from me and pounded me
with there Fists something feerse. Everybody was
yelling and shouting and some of the women in the
Crowd was screaming. I shut my eyes and tryed to put
my hands over my head but the soljers wouldnt let me.
When they finally stopped beating on me I opened my
eyes and seen Mister Weaver and his Son standing over

on the side of the street like they was turned to Stone but I seen no sign of Dundee. He was gone like a Ghost and who could blame him seeing by how much he was outnumbered.

Take him to jail Lutenant Nordell ordered. The soljers dragged me down the street and they threw me in jail just like they had been told to do.

Even though I hurt all over I lay on my bunk in my cell and was glad at how things had turned out on account of the lie I had told to the Lutenant about it being me who had shot Major Parkinson and not Dundee.

I was glad on account of I had finally evened up the score between Dundee and me. He had saved my life that time at the dance when the Jayhawker that had been molesting Louise Stokes set out to shoot me and now I had done him the same Favor.

I was also glad that Dundee being the smart man he was seen his chanse and made his get away while all those soljers was pownsing on me and beating me within an inch of my life. I imajined him off somewhere right then riding tall in the Saddle maybe on his way to California to see the oshun.

Two days later they taken me to Tryal. They had a Judge and a Jury and they had Witnesses mostly soljers but some regular folk to who all said yes they had seen me shoot Major Parkinson down in cold Blood. I got up and said I never said I didnt do it which made the lawyer they had give me pitch a Fit.

The Judge said I was guilty and that I would have to hang the very next day.

Once I was back in my cell I tryed not to dwell on that last part and Miss Cordelia coming to visit me helped on that score.

She brought me some biskuts with Apple Butter spred on them and they sure did taste good.

Why did you do it Jubal she asked me and it was on the tip of my Tongue to tell the Truth and say I didnt do it it was Dundee did it. But insted I ansered I did it on account of I had to defend myself like we all did. If I had told her the Truth that it was Dundee shot Major Parkinson it might have made her think less of him than she did and I didnt want that to happen. It didnt matter what she thought about me.

I asked her was her Father and her brother well and she said they were and they send you there best regards. I told her tell them thank you for that.

Then I asked her about what was most on my mind and she told me no she hadnt seen Dundee and didnt have any idea where he was. She told me her Father and her brother said they hadnt seen what happened to Dundee while the shooting was going on but they reckoned he had rode away sinse they couldnt find his horse when all the excitement was finally over and done with.

Dont worry I said to Miss Cordelia he will come back to you once things settle down some.

She heeved a sigh and said I hope so.

Then we talked about would it rain or not before night and finally she said oh Jubal I hope you will understand but I will not be there tomorrow when its time because I simply could not bear to see you

She give a little sob without finishing what she had ment to say and then she called for the Sherriff and he come and let her leave.

Not long after Miss Cordelia had gone a man from the town newspaper he said was called the Advocate come to my cell. The Sherriff let him in. He said he

wanted to tell my story in the weekly Advocate which
was to come out the next morning. He said it would
make a good story for the last time the Advocate was
to be published on account of he was leaving town for
good once he had printed it up and given it out to the
boys who sold it on the streets.

I got no story to tell I told him but he asked me a lot
of Questions about where was I born and who was my
parents and how come I was in Missouri shooting at
soljers and what made me murder Major Parkinson.

I ansered him as best I could except for that last part
which had me by the tail. I couldnt tell him that
Dundee was the murderer not me.

He wrote down all my ansers and then he went
away leaving me alone again.

The morning come way to soon to suit me. I made
up my mind to be brave but while I was waiting for
them to come to fetch me I had to get the Sherriff to
take me out back to the outhouse Three times in just a
few minnits.

Then I wrote in the Journal where I had been
writing about Dundee THE END and stuck the
Journal in my pocket.

But it werent THE END and why it werent is what
I am going to try to write down now before it is to late
to write anything more.

Here is what happened then.

The Sherriff come and he taken me out my cell and
he marched me to the Gallows and up its steps. They
was looping the Noose around my neck and tieing my
hands behind my back when Lutenant Nordell come
out the crowd that had come to see me hang. He shook
a Fist at me and called me all kinds of bad names. He
said I was the skum of the earth for what I had done to

Major Parkinson who he said was the finest man and greatest soljer who ever lived. He said hanging was to good for me and now that Dundee werent around to look out for me he ment to cook my Goose good. With that he pulled out his gun and he shot me in the gut.

Folk started screaming. The Sherriff took to cussing. I heard them from where I lay on the Gallows platform bleeding like a stuck Pig.

Thats when Dundee come riding up with Mister Bantry. Without a word he pulled out his gun and he shot Lutenant Nordell in plain sight of everybody there to keep him from shooting me again like he was fixing to do. Then him and Mister Bantry come up on the Gallows platform. Dundee looked down at me and then he yelled somebody go fetch the Doctor for this man. He didnt say boy. He said man.

Then he bent down and took the noose off of my neck and I said howdy where have you been.

Chasing down Asa Bantry he said and the Sherriff said what for and Dundee said on account of I seen Bantry shoot Major Parkinson in that fracas that took place here awhile back. I went after him and though he give me the slip One or Two times I finally caught him and here he is Sherriff for you to take to Tryal.

I couldnt beleeve my ears.

Why would Bantry shoot Major Parkinson the Sherriff asked suspishusly.

Tell him Dundee said to Mister Bantry and Mister Bantry said he let his soljers set fire to our homeplace. They took my wife with them after beating me senseless. I found out where they were camped in Kansas. I went there and found Three Soljers burying April. They laughed and said they had all had her. They said they didnt know what she dyed of the night after Major Parkinson and his men set out to come up here to hunt for Dundee. I killed all Three of them and then I come up here after Parkinson. When the shooting started the other day I joined in and got him on my first shot. You can hang me but I tell you True I would do it all over again if I had the chanse for Aprils sake and for the sake of the Child she was carrying and never mind that I would have to die for the doing of the Deed.

The Sherriff taken Mister Bantry down off of the Gallows platform and out of sight. Dundee propped me up and stayed with me until the Doctor come and looked me over and said make him comfortable thats all we can do for him at this point.

I had known before the Doctor said what he did that I was a goner. I could feel it like a Shrowd slipping over me. I could hardly feel any pain even. I just felt sort of groggy and not on account of how I had slept so fretfull the night before I knew. It kept getting harder and harder to write things down in my Journal. But I werent afraid not with Dundee right there beside me.

I said to him I thought all along it was you who killed the Major.

So why did you jump in with both feet and claim you had done it he asked me. What ever in the world made you do a dam fool thing like that.

You saved my life once I said so I owed you. I wanted to pay you back in kind for what you did for me.

I knew you hadnt killed Parkinson Dundee said. I seen Asa draw a beed on Parkinson and shoot him in the head. When Nordell threw down on you and then the both of us couldnt light out of there together on account of how Nordell had his men jump you I reckoned that I had best be on my way after Asa who I saw ride out right after he had killed Parkinson. I hadnt bargained on it taking me so long to run him to ground which got me back here with him to late to stop Nordell from shooting you.

I appreciate what you did for me I said and I did. That it didnt work out wasnt something I could bring myself to fault Dundee for. He done his best for me.

Dundee said I planned on forsing Asa to confess to the killing if I had to to get you off the hook. Dammit if I hadnt lost his trail twise I would have got back here in time and everything would have been Hunky Dory.

Is Lutenant Nordell dead I asked and Dundee ansered yes he is.

I wonder would you do me a Favor I said. When Dundee said you bet I would I asked him would he keep my Journal once I was gone. I told him it would be allright should he want to read it some time. He held out his hand to take it from me but I said no not yet.

I could hear the newsboys hawking the Advocate. I could hear them calling out to people to read all about how Jubal Bonner had Murdered Major James Parkinson and been hanged for the Crime. But it was way to late for me to do any thing about that though it saddened me to think that if folk come upon that newspaper years after things had all blown over and settled down they would beleeve that what was wrote in it was true about how I was supposed to have shot Major Parkinson to death.

When I felt my hands and feet going cold I looked up from my writing at Dundee and said it looks like we just wasnt ment to be together for long.

I guess not he said. But it was nothing if not fine the little time we lasted wasnt it he said and I said it sure was.

He tryed to give me a grin then and I let on like I never seen the Tears in his eyes.

I knew that was just about all I had time to write down about a man named Dundee except that it had been real good to know him and

ABOUT THE AUTHOR

Leo P. Kelley has read and traveled widely, and his writing reflects his wide-ranging experience. He is the author of several Westerns, including the popular Luke Sutton series. His most recent Double D Western is *Luke Sutton: Hired Gun.*

only copy in my system

CAZENOVIA PUBLIC LIBRARY

100 Albany Street
Cazenovia, N.Y. 13035

(315) 655-9322

MEMBER

MID-YORK LIBRARY SYSTEM
Utica, N.Y. 13502